PALADINE

KENNETH EADE

To George Gonzalez, First Sergeant, Ret., the inspiration behind this remarkable character

"Whenever men take the law into their own hands, the loser is the law. And when the law loses, freedom languishes."
– Robert Kennedy

FOREWORD

I know about war and how it is waged at the operational and tactical levels. I served 22 years as an active duty soldier in the United States Army. After retiring with honors due to medical reasons I continued to serve the Department of the Army as a civilian. I held various positions starting as an Operations Officer in a Logistics Operation Center, a Battle Captain, and then as the Chief of Operations. I also served as a Process Improvement Specialist and ended my career as a Logistics Strategic Planning Analyst. In all I served the Army for 34 years.

On 11 September 2001, while stationed at Fort Sill, Oklahoma I watched the terrorist attack on the twin towers on television as did all Americans, and the entire world. We witnessed the horror of terrorism and knew in our hearts that life, as we knew it, would never be the same. Being a New Yorker it hit as close to home as if I had been in actual combat. As a soldier I also thought: "We must now change the way we fight. We will also need a new breed of soldier to do whatever must be done to ensure what I am looking at will never happen again." In Kenneth Eade's book "Paladine" Mr.

1

Eade gives us one of the "new breed," former soldier Robert Garcia.

In reality men like Robert have been used by the United States' intelligence community as far back as the mid-eighties. The American government was fearful of what was happening in Central America with the Sandinistas in power in Nicaragua and with El Salvador mired in internal conflict which lasted into the early 90s. The domino principle came into play. Since Nicaragua fell to the communists how much longer before Honduras falls, then Guatemala, El Salvador...

The 'Vietnam Syndrome' was the phrase used to define the American citizens' hesitation to involve our country in foreign affairs. The public refused to send its young men and women into war again so soon after the Vietnam debacle, fought by the brave military personnel whose names adorn the Vietnam Memorial. Yet, the American intelligence organizations showed no hesitation at all. They recruited, trained, and deployed that new breed around the world to ensure America's strategic interests were protected by any means necessary.

In this book Kenneth Eade takes you through a chapter in the life of Robert Garcia, a character originally introduced in Kenneth's book, "Beyond All Recognition." Garcia was formerly Malik Abdul who rose to existence when US Army Captain John Richards was called upon to sacrifice all that he knew, all that he loved to serve his beloved country and its corps. He was a patriot of the highest order and when he came out of the cold to help a former commander, a fellow soldier, he became persona non grata, a man who held too many secrets in his head, secrets that Pennsylvania Avenue wanted to keep hidden from the world. He was marked.

What happens to men like Robert Garcia when they are no longer in the field, when the rush of combat is no longer available, when the country they love and have fought for is no longer a safe haven? There is no 'on/off' switch for these highly trained individuals. They have been given a rash by their handlers, a rash with a constant itch that can only be relieved by doing what they do best. They must create their own agenda to survive. In the absence of targets previously given to them by the agency they must create their own. They were made by desperate men for desperate times and now will not simply go away into that good night. They are the government's nightmare. Simply put, they are America's assassins.

This is a work of fiction based on extensive research by Kenneth Eade. He hits the mark. Men like Robert Garcia exist, their dossiers spread across the desks of nervous intelligence directors. Enjoy the book and give thanks you're not in Robert's crosshairs.

First Sergeant George Gonzalez (Ret)
US Army

CHAPTER ONE

The apartment obviously belonged to a bachelor, but it was neat and orderly, like a military man's freshly made bed. The cushions on the couch were soft and comfortable and the Colonial style furniture practical and functional, rustic but not antique. The décor was earth tone and neutral, and the walls were peppered with tasteful framed prints, replicas of art that said nothing about the occupant. They were just hanging there so the walls would not be bare. There were no framed family photos on the tables, no stacks of well-worn books and no magazines. It was almost as if nobody lived there.

Robert Garcia finished putting all his essential things in his backpack and took one last look around, not for sentiment, but to make sure he left no evidence of his real identity behind. He was an unremarkable man. Other men, the exceptional types, could never be forgotten. Men of striking, imposing persuasion, or those with a certain superior intellect or cleverness. Robert held none of those attributes but, if you had the misfortune to have him touch your life in any way, and were fortuitous enough to live after the experience, he would be indelibly etched in your memory.

Robert's characteristics were fine-drawn, precise. He could drift in on the night air with only a whisper of the wind, and then disappear into the shadows, the only place where he ever felt secure and content. At five-foot-eleven, dark-haired

5

with a touch of grey around the edges, he was a chameleon that blended in with most crowds. But under the ordinary clothing he wore he had the body of a herculean powerhouse, chiseled and ripped. Née John Richards, Jr. to an American military career man who had taken a Lebanese wife. Since Robert had been old enough to walk, he had marched in the footsteps of his father, a military man. When his country came calling, John Richards, Jr. proudly answered that call and served with pride as his father's son, the nephew of his Great Uncle Sam. There was never any question of it. Working up the ranks the hard way, he made Captain, and it wasn't long before his special traits and abilities landed him his first secret assignment, along with his first alias – Malik Abdul.

Malik was a name that had fit Robert well. He never did look or behave like a John Richards. That was a name his Anglo Father, John Richards, Sr., had insisted on giving the child and his mother dutifully went along with it. Eventually, it was adept profiling that helped Malik recognize his destiny. His swarthy skin and his second language – Arabic – made Malik a valuable asset to his country. Beyond his language prowess and physical attributes, Malik possessed a unique set of special skills, forged by intensive training and honed to perfection with experience. Malik and his band of assassins were utilized only in the most extreme of circumstances – covert operations for well-known agencies who called themselves by three-letter acronyms – and the unknown ones as well.

He had tried to retire, tried his hand at transforming his life into the "normal" one of Robert Garcia, and had dutifully taken the number 4 train Monday through Friday, from his little apartment in El Barrio to Two Penn Plaza, where he worked at a "regular job." But Malik's past had beckoned. It was a call he could not resist. He had come out into the open to testify for a fellow soldier in a court-martial trial who had been given a bum rap. About the only thing Malik had left which resembled a conscience was the soldier's creed. He had no morals, no principles, except for those which were burned into his hardwiring like a brand on a cow: The mission comes first; never accept defeat; never quit; and *never leave a fallen comrade*.

Robert had come back from the court-martial trial on the coast a ball of nerves, constantly looking over his shoulder. Now that the record had been set straight, Robert's life was in a state of distress and disquietude.

I can't go back to the job. They're probably watching for me there.

Robert also couldn't return to the woman he had been seeing regularly, and who had given him hope that he actually could rejoin society after all that he had seen and done, and he couldn't go back to this quaint little brownstone on 118th Street, between 2nd and 3rd Avenues in Spanish Harlem that he had called home for the past five years.

I only have to come back one last time, he thought, as he shut the door behind him.

***

Now that Robert had exposed himself and his new identity to set the record straight it was, once again, time to slide back into the shadows. Without a glimpse of emotion, he left everything behind that he had collected over the years –the furniture, the clothing, the little knick-knacks reminiscent of the life he had simulated. He also left something in the apartment that had never been there before, a product of his life's work – something that he had not produced for the past five years – the body of a dead man, five-foot-eleven, olive-skinned and dark-haired, a dead-ringer for Robert. He took one last look at the life of Robert Garcia as he threw the match on the floor and then slipped away.

CHAPTER TWO

Robert checked his wallet and leafed through the bills that he had saved up.

Need to think, need a plan.

No operation, including the one he called his own life, could ever move forward without one. His stash would only last so long, and he would need money. He had spent a good chunk of the currency he had saved on his new driver's license and passport. He pondered the idea of using the passport to go to war zones or conflict areas – anywhere he could pick up some mercenary work – the kind of jobs he was really good at.

Robert looked at the passport and chuckled as he thought of his new name – Julio Ignacio.

Sounds like two first names.

Now that he had a Spanish name, he made a mental note to perfect his Spanish, and considered his next move as he sat in the orange, molded plastic bench, hunched over his Big Mac at the greasy, sticky orange table at McDonald's.

It was the busiest hour of the day, full of the laughter and shrieking of children, the wailing of babies, and the shuffling of businesspeople trying to fit a quick bite into their busy workday. He watched a young mother push her toddler down into his seat and spoon-feed him bites of a hamburger while he was playing with the action figure that came with the happy meal.

Another baby was crying and banging the metal tray of his high chair, but Robert only heard one sound, – the metallic click of a weapon being cocked back.

In a fraction of a second, in one well-oiled motion, Robert withdrew his 9mm Glock, which he kept on his person at all times, turned in the direction of the sound with lightning speed, and fired three shots at the young man standing between the glass doors who was holding an AK-47 assault rifle aimed at the crowd – one in head and two in the chest. The man crumpled to the floor before he was able to shout "Allahu Akbar" and the AK-47 clacked down in front of his lifeless body.

Amid the screams and frantic movements of the throng, Robert again slipped away into oblivion. He would soon discover there would be no need to think about a plan anymore – in that one twist of fate, it had been made for him.

**

While the conventional news media was trying to get a handle on what had happened, dozens of people were texting and tweeting their version of what they had witnessed. Instagrams of the dead terrorist and videos of his body on the floor with the assault rifle in front of it went viral.

The final story was pieced together from bloggers, who reported that the attempted "McDonald's massacre" had been foiled by a miracle man, a lone, armed soldier who had somehow spotted the 22 year old terrorist, neutralized him before he could deliver his deadly payload, and slipped away like a super hero without claiming any of the accolades. Internet reports melded with the eyewitness accounts and social media gossip. The mysterious rescuer was hailed as a hero, a paladin in the urban folklore culture of the Millennials, whose minds infused what most people knew as real with the virtual reality of video gaming.

Robert's identity was unknown, but that didn't stop a prominent blogger from giving him the name of: Paladine. It was an honorable name, but Robert didn't deserve it. In the underground pop culture of the lost generation, a paladin was a holy knight, a class of warrior that was fully devoted to kindness and ridding the universe of evil. Paladins are said to fear nothing because evil fears them. That much may have been true about Robert, but he would never be this person, this Paladine. He would never be the man in the white hat or the knight in shining armor. A warrior, yes, that he was, but he could not be one of the "good guys." Robert had seen too much, done too much. Killing had turned into just a way of life for Robert. He simply killed whomever his instincts told him to. He had tried to fit into society, and what did it do for him? He was disillusioned and discouraged, and that made him even more dangerous than he normally was. Robert was an assassin, plain and simple, a killer who could waste five police officers while going after his target without batting an eye and chalk it up to "collateral damage."

But there was something else that made Robert even more treacherous. He had this itch that he had not scratched in a very long while. With the McDonald's shooter, Robert had scratched that itch until it had festered and burned, and now the only remedy was to kill again.

CHAPTER THREE

The conference room at the NCTC, the National Counterterrorism Center in McLean, Virginia, was filled with the suited chiefs of the "who's who" of government alphabet soup – the heads of the NSA, CIA, FBI, Department of Homeland Security and Department of Defense were all there. The only one missing was the president, who had issued an order to examine the nation's readiness against "homegrown" terrorist attacks, and the McDonald's attack was right on the top of the list. Getting them to talk to one another was no small task for NCTC Director Nathan Anderson.

Anderson did not look like any of his acronymic counterparts. Except for his G-Man style grey suit, which one usually expected to see worn by an FBI agent, he could have passed for a businessman in any executive office in New York. He was a career bureaucrat who had come originally from the State Department, and had served in various capacities at the center since its inception after 9/11. He had also done a stint advising the president and the National

Security Council on counterterrorism. Under Anderson, the agency had built the best database of suspected terrorists in the world, but there was one problem with it – they could not go after terrorists themselves. They had no enforcement capability. All they could do was pass the data on to appropriate enforcement agencies, like the FBI and the CIA, who considered the NCTC to be superfluous, and Anderson no more than a data manager.

Tall and with an imposing frame, Anderson had a permanently serious look on his face. After all, his work was vital and indispensable to the security of the United States of America, and he felt emasculated to have all this data and be powerless to do anything with it. Once again, in the meeting, he tried to impress upon his colleagues the need to make regular use of the data to sweep up suspected terrorists for questioning and step up surveillance. The McDonald's attack showed that the United States was vulnerable to the so-called "homegrown" lone-wolf terrorist attacks, where, instead of being planned by ISIS or Al-Qaeda, a young, recently radicalized jihadist would take matters in his own hands to kill as many infidels as he possibly could, finishing the act with his own death. Traditional law enforcement methods did not encompass looking for and apprehending these new domestic jihadists, who were either recruited by or answered the 2014 call of ISIS to:

"Kill any salibis you can find. You can use anything. For example, a car. Process your target. The bigger the better. But if it's difficult, it's more important in jihad to simplify it and to do it sooner… Video the process. Run over them while passing… If you can kill a disbelieving American or European – especially the spiteful and filthy French – or an Australian, or a Canadian, or any other disbeliever … including the citizens of the countries that entered into a coalition against the Islamic State, then rely upon Allah, and kill him in any manner or way however it may be."

"Didn't you have a file on this kid – Abdul Moussef?" asked Bill Carpenter, Director of the FBI.

Anderson sighed, and ran his hand through his grey moustache and beard, then shook an accusatory hand at the group. "That's the problem with our procedures, Bill. We *do* have a report on Moussef and it went out to *everybody*, including the FBI and local law enforcement in New York. He's listed in TIDE[1] and in your own TSDB[2]."

That accusatory hand came crashing down on the table.

"God damn it, doesn't anyone pay attention to these things?"

Anderson could see that his outburst was not well taken. Each of the men at the table had been appointed by the president, and each thought his own job to be the most important. They did not take kindly to being criticized by a man they considered to be nothing more than a data collector.

As the meeting proceeded, Anderson became more and more impatient. This show and tell wasn't going to help him with his directive – to lead the nation's effort to combat terrorism and integrate all instruments of national power to ensure unity of effort. Pointing fingers and passing the buck were not going to ensure any kind of unity – only dissension.

"You got anything on this 'Paladine' fella?" asked Carpenter.

"Our databases are coming up with nothing. He's a ghost."

---

[1] Terrorist Identities Datamart Environment

[2] Terrorist Screening Database

"Well, he's a ghost we have to catch. We don't want vigilantes out there running around with guns, shooting down suspected terrorists. We'll get him. I've got my best agents assigned to the job."

"With all due respect, Bill, he did you guys a favor." Anderson bit his lower lip. They just couldn't change their mindset. To them, the "case" was Paladine, the murderer of a young jihadist – never mind that he had prevented the murder of dozens of innocents – instead of the next terrorist, lurking out there, with his finger on the trigger or detonator switch, waiting to make his next deadly move. That's how the FBI worked, on a case-by-case basis. In the war on terrorism, Anderson felt a more broad-stroke approach was warranted.

***

Bryce Williamson had built his empire from the ground up. He had invested well, weathered all the major financial crises of the late 20th and early 21st centuries, and was able to retire a rich man. His $30 million penthouse apartment in the city of San Francisco was ultra-modern, but garnished with classical French and Italian furniture that had been purchased from Christie's and Sotheby's. Once handcrafted for royalty, the richly ornamented antiques from the Ancient Regime of varnished wood and sleek, slender, delicate legs were works of art in and of themselves. To match the period, on his walls hung the true artistic masterpieces of Van Gogh, Monet and Pissarro. Hidden in a masterfully hand-painted cabinet was an instrument that tied Williamson's furnishings to the modern world – a television, which was spewing out entertainment called "news." All the talk was about the mysterious vigilante they were calling: *Paladine*.

Williamson's ears perked to the story as he attempted to drown his sorrows with shots of expensive scotch. This had been his pastime since retiring. That and a long battle with lung cancer, to which he had eventually gracefully conceded.

Williamson had reached a pinnacle in his professional and financial life, only to find that he had nobody to share that wealth, or life, with. His only son, John, had died in a horrible terrorist attack in San Francisco in 2006. His beloved flesh and blood, the heir to his legacy, had been wiped out by a jihadist who had run down a bunch of people on a crowded San Francisco sidewalk. Bryce couldn't cope with the loss and it didn't take long for grief to turn to outrage. He pulled all his well-paid strings for action – the police, his congressman, even his local senator – but the scum who killed his son was found not guilty by reason of insanity and was now languishing in a state mental hospital instead of the gas chamber. Bryce's anger, like his cancer, had metastasized and incensed him to the point of action. Others, his peers, had amassed great wealth and had created their own charitable foundations. *Start a cancer foundation! Do something good for the world!* They all had told him the same thing. Coughing, he pushed the glass away, grabbed the remote control, and flipped around, searching for more news reports about the foiled McDonald's' attack and the mysterious, elusive Paladine.

Bryce turned his attention to the screen. The news commentator, an above-average looking woman, was summarizing the comments from ISIS about the stymied McDonald's attack. She was interpreting the videotaped comments of the ISIS spokesman, who said Abdul Moussef was a hero, a martyr, and called upon every jihadist to kill as many American infidels as possible. He also vowed that they would hunt down, crucify and behead the one known as Paladine. Williamson decided right then and there what legacy he would leave to the world, while at the same time extracting his revenge against the killer of his son and his mentors.

CHAPTER FOUR

Robert Garcia holed up in an apartment hotel in Harlem that didn't have a guest register, which was managed by a heavily armed ex-soldier whose conscience had joined Robert's in Never Never Land. He had taken one look at Robert and understood his need for privacy without asking. The hotel was a dive, but next door there was an Internet café that Robert could hack into.

Robert was pissed off. He couldn't stand the fact that he had spent his military career fighting these filthy jihadists and now they were right in his own backyard.

They need to be taught a lesson.

He stewed as he sat on the yellowed mattress in his small, roach infested studio, with the black and white TV on in the background. A reporter was talking about the McDonald's terrorist, so he turned his attention to the report.

The mysterious savior has been dubbed by social media sources as "Paladine."

Suddenly, he had an epiphany. Robert had to descend into the bowels of the Darknet, the cyber-haven of drug dealers and child pornography peddlers, whose currency was the untraceable Bitcoin. Robert didn't dare use the traditional Internet. The feds would surely be looking for his cyber fingerprint. The Darknet was his domain, where he could do his research and send messages encrypted in layers. Those messages would travel through a series of anonymous routers and their origination would be forever unknown because an investigator would only know the location of the router before and after the current layer. The message was decrypted only on the receiver's side using a PGP, or public key.

Armed with his impeccable Arabic, he trolled the blogs, chat rooms, and Twitter and Facebook pages of the virtual caliphate, watching beheading and crucifixion videos and skimming the radical Islamic sermons of the jihadist movement. He created an Islamic handle for himself as "Jamal," the Muslim immigrant from Jordan who was curious how he could do his part in the global jihadist movement without having to move to Syria. It didn't take long for an ISIS recruiter to contact him, and point out a place where he could learn more about the jihadist philosophy.

***

The place was the Islamic Academy in Bay Ridge, in a mosque which had been established by the North Atlantic Islamic Trust, which had long been suspected of providing bases of operation of jihadists, and whose several facilities had in fact harbored terrorists. To look the part, Robert had trimmed his dark, curly beard and shaped it like a boomerang around his chin, jihadist style. When Robert arrived, he passed all his initiation examinations in his perfect Arabic under the watchful eye of a radical Islamic cleric, and then was invited to attend a discussion group in the basement of the mosque that treaded the thin line between Islamism and terrorism, which was led by a 20-something Saudi who appeared to be the oldest person in the room, except for Robert.

Talk was buzzing around martyrdom, the McDonald's attack and their new hated enemy – Paladine. The discussion then focused on whether a suicide bombing would have been more effective than an attack with an automatic weapon. The Saudi explained that the message of Islam was that it wasn't important how many infidels you took out. You should try to kill as many as possible, but even if you took the life of only one infidel, you would be a martyr and have a permanent place with Allah in Jannah. It also wasn't crucial what type of weapon you chose. Robert volunteered his opinion.

"Either way, you end up dead."

One of the boys, who looked no more than 18, stood up and got in Robert's face.

"What's this to you, old man? What do you know about it?"

"I know plenty. Who's your leader here, this guy?" Robert motioned with his head cocked toward the Saudi guy.

The Saudi replied, "Our only leader is God. I am a teacher."

"Oh, so you're a teacher?" Robert's bearded face broke out in an evil grin. "And this is the kind of horse shit you think is right to teach to these young impressionable minds? Promising them a better life after they off themselves? Death is just death. There's no Jannah, and I can prove it to you." The boys looked at Robert in shock as he focused his expressionless, shark-like eyes on the teacher. "I've got a math problem for you, teacher." Robert pulled out his gun from his shoulder holster and panned it in front of the startled participants. "How many of you lunatic jihadists can I send to meet your God with this one little gun?" He pulled and waved his Glock at them and cocked his head to one side and smiled. Then he took aim, shot the teacher in the head and killed him instantly. "Tell your other teachers Paladine sends his regards." Robert backed out of the room, moving the pistol from boy to boy as they covered their faces and screamed in horror.

Robert knew he needed to leave New York, and immediately. He descended into the subterranean underworld of the New York subway, ducked into a bathroom, wiped the gun clean and disposed of it by burying it deep in the trash can. Then he headed for Penn Station. There, he paid cash for a ticket to Chicago. If he decided to go further from there, he would buy another ticket in Chicago on another day. Long-term trips were too easy to trace.

***

The intern knocked on the door of Nathan Anderson's private office at NCTC.

"Come in."

The young lady smiled, and left a memo on his desk.

"Thank you." Anderson looked at the memo and frowned. Another jihadist from the TIDE database had been assassinated, and this time the shooter left a calling card – Paladine. He put out an alert to all domestic and international agencies NCTC was intended to serve. Paladine, whomever he was, had to be identified and apprehended.

CHAPTER FIVE

Bryce Williamson had finally found his charitable inspiration. He summoned his lawyers and created the *John Williamson Foundation to Fight Terrorism*. On the surface, it was a normal, legitimate charitable institution. But in the substratum depths of its understructure, it had an opprobrious purpose – to kill every suspected terrorist who lurked in every sleeper cell in America, beginning with the so-called "insane" jihadist who mowed down his son in 2006 and who was relaxing in a mental hospital instead of waiting on death row where he belonged. Williamson made a sizeable contribution to the foundation himself, and then called upon everyone who had ever benefited from an association with him in business to contribute. Most of his former associates donated with only a modicum of persuasion. Others he coerced into it with friendly extortion. Throughout his many years of business, Bryce had come to know where all the bodies were buried. When he received a negative or non-enthusiastic answer, he simply gently resorted to blackmail. This local politician had taken bribes; therefore he must contribute. Want that evidence of toxic waste cover-up for construction of your high-rise apartments to remain under wraps? Pitch in. If the object of the shakedown threatened to expose Williamson's role in it, he had a simple and ironclad defense – he was going to die and he didn't give a shit.

He put his formerly busy legislative lawyers to work on drafting bills to put into the hands of the unscrupulous senators and congressmen who had taken payoffs. It was pay-back time. The laws were archaic and did not allow federal enforcement agencies to prevent terrorism, only to prosecute accused terrorists. Those laws had to be changed.

Williamson put his webmasters to work on developing a beautiful website for the foundation. No expense was spared. Journalists who had been compelled to "work for food," peddling each of their articles to the mainstream publications which would still pay, were employed on the foundation's payroll to research and write about counterterrorism and prevention. The Editor-in-Chief, of course, was Bryce Williamson himself. But beneath that legitimate online iceberg, lurking in the stinking depths of the Dark web, was the "other" website, the subversive one which could only be accessed through the TOR onion router. This site offered articles recommending counterterrorism prevention. Some writers even postulated assassination of suspected terrorists. Bryce intended to build an army and he wanted Paladine to be his general.

CHAPTER SIX

It had been a while since Robert had been on a hunt and he was getting restless. He didn't like Chicago that much. The pizza pie was okay, but they called it a "deep dish" – not a pie. He missed drifting through the New York street crowd, selecting hypothetical victims, plotting the murders in his mind and his subsequent getaway into the shadows. He was running out of money and he spent his nights surfing the sewers of the deep web, looking for potential employment. Finally, he latched on to a website called "CounterTerror.onion," What had caught his eye was an article that praised Paladine and advocated assassination of all suspected terrorist cells in America and Western Europe. The article was anonymous, but contained a PGP Public Key contact for the journalist who had written it.

Robert composed an encrypted message to the author of the article, asking for more information on how he could get involved, then went off to grab a late dinner. When he returned with his "deep dish" pie, he checked his PGP and, to his surprise, he found a response. It said simply: *Are you Paladine?*

***

Communicating with encrypted messages using the TOR browser was frustratingly slow. The site had no chat rooms. In fact, there were a limited number of them on the Darknet. Robert responded back with: "Are you a cop?" All kinds of law enforcement agencies were known to prowl the Darknet in cyber undercover. After several days of overly circumspect back and forth messages on both sides, a meeting was arranged. It would be on Williamson's home turf but on Robert's terms.

Robert prepared his black knapsack as a go-bag with his stash of cash, three prepaid cellular phones, two prepaid credit cards, a small pillow, a blanket and some other essentials. He dressed in black jeans and a black shirt, shoved a knitted black winter hat into the pocket of his black jacket, holstered his new 9mm Glock and strapped the Ruger SR22 onto his ankle. He slung the backpack over his shoulder and stepped out of the hotel room.

Robert was a good two days ahead of schedule for the meeting with the anonymous contact from the website who was known to him simply as "B." He wanted to prepare for the rendezvous and set the layout so that there would be no surprises. In Robert's business, one surprise could be fatal. The train yard in Chicago was filled with infrared cameras and heat sensors, so Robert decided to hop the train outside the yard, while it was still building up speed. He didn't want to have to shoot anyone who tried to ruin his travel experience – that would destroy the entire idea of traveling anonymously.

For the next two days, Robert rode the rails, leaving not even a trail of bread crumbs to follow. As the train decelerated on its way into the San Francisco train yard, Robert jumped off and silently drifted away from it like a thin coat of fog, blending into the night air. When Robert had cleared the yard, he whipped off his mask and stuffed it into his backpack. No need to call attention to himself. He was also unlikely to hitch a ride from anyone if he was dressed like a burglar.

Robert hit the highway with his thumb outstretched. It took a while, so he walked along the road, munching on some peanuts from his bag. Finally, a beat-up, old white 70s-era Chevrolet Impala chugged over to the side. Robert trotted up to the passenger side window, which was rolling down.

"Where ya headed?" A beefy white man with a shiny bald head and a thick grey beard cocked his head through the window and smiled at Robert.

"San Francisco."

The beefy guy motioned with his tank-topped arm. "Well, hop in then, buddy."

Robert opened the door, tossed his pack into the well of the passenger's seat, sat down and closed the door.

"What's your name?" asked the beefy guy as the Impala puffed up dirt from the shoulder. Robert thought for a split second.

"You can call me Bill."

A smile of yellow, crooked teeth broke out beneath the beefy guy's beard. "That's my name!"

Robert held out his fist for a pump and the real Bill tapped it.

"You a vet?"

"How did you know?"

"You got the look. Plus, I know the train yard is just a couple miles away from here. I pick up a lot of vets on this route. 18th Cavalry, National Guard."

"22nd Infantry Regiment."

"Regular Army?"

"Yeah."

"You must have seen action in Iraq."

"More than I care to talk about or recall."

"Understood. Well, it's good to have a brother in my car. We should be in the city in about a half hour. I'm headed toward the Embarcadero."

"That suits me just fine."

Bill shook out a pack of cigarettes, pulled the top off with his teeth and tapped it on his brawny biceps. He popped out a filter tip and offered it to Robert.

"No thanks, don't smoke."

"Smart man."

Beefy Bill didn't know the half of it.

CHAPTER SEVEN

Robert let a room at the Bradley Hotel on Pine Street. It was not too dirty, and he was able to check in by turning over three "Ben Franklin" IDs. That brought the cost of the room up to $342 for the first night. Robert figured he would only need it for two at the most. After getting his key, he went outside on recon to explore the lay of the land and set the area for his meeting. Robert knew he wanted the meeting to be downtown, so he rode the cable cars to select the perfect spot. He found that place at a little restaurant in Chinatown. It was off the beaten path, had a small number of tables, a glass front so he could observe the goings-on outside, a quick back exit through the kitchen and very good dim-sum.

Robert walked the route he had plotted out to lead up to the meeting. Cable cars were a perfect mode of transportation because they were slow and Robert could follow along and observe the car while at the same time concealing himself in the crowd. He purchased four prepaid cellular telephones at a Walgreens and continued to plot his course. Finally, everything was as perfect as a plan could possibly be, which did not guarantee that anything or everything could not go wrong, so Robert went over it again and again in his mind.

***

Robert held the disposable cell phone up to his lips. "Hello, B, are you ready for our little rendezvous?"

Bryce Williamson was shocked. Could this be Paladine? If so, he was better than he had thought.

"How did you get this number?"

"The only number not traceable is one that doesn't belong to you. Something to remember. Now, I want you to listen carefully, because I won't be repeating this."

"I will, I will."

"Good. At the front desk in your building, you'll find a message from me. Don't tell anybody about this. If I see you talking to anyone, all bets are off."

"Can you see me?"

"No questions. First step is to go and get that message. Next, take it back to the apartment and read it."

"Now? But it's one in the morning."

"Yes, now."

Robert focused his night vision goggles on the lobby of Williamson's building from his comfortable spot in the shadows. Five minutes later, Williamson appeared at his concierge's desk in a brown bathrobe.

Probably has his initials monogrammed on it.

Robert watched carefully as Williamson took the package containing the message and a disposable cell phone.

Back upstairs, Williamson closed the door of his apartment and ripped open the manila envelope. He dropped the mobile phone onto his desk and unfolded the paper that had been wrapped around it. The note, written with a laser printer, read:

Don't use this phone in your apartment. It is not safe. Don't even turn it on until you are out. Tomorrow afternoon at 12 pm, get on the cable car at the California Street end of the line. Then, turn on the phone. Don't turn it on before that time. I will be in touch. Now take this message into the bathroom and, with a cigarette lighter, burn it over the toilet and flush the ashes.

Bryce did as he was instructed. He coughed and sputtered as he burned the message, then hacked up some phlegm and spit it into the toilet before he flushed the ashes. He scrambled to the medicine cabinet, withdrew a package of valium and took 10 milligrams. There would be no sleeping without it.

As Bryce settled into his king-size bed, Robert walked the meeting route backwards to the point of its origin. When he was satisfied, he headed back to the Bradley Hotel. Tomorrow marked the first day of his new career, or the end of life as he knew it.

CHAPTER EIGHT

Robert Garcia spotted Bryce Williamson waiting in line at the California Street cable car turntable and scanned the area for others who may be observing him. He dialed the number of the throwaway cell phone.

"You're doing good, B. Get on the second car and call me when you're moving."

Bryce coughed and sputtered. He was a little frustrated because the first car had not taken off yet and the second would not be moving for a while, but he waited as he had been told. As the first car began to move, Robert streaked out of the crowd, hopped on the side of it and held on to a handrail. He rode the car all the way to Montgomery Street and jumped off.

The second car was finally packed up and began to move. Bryce extracted the gifted phone from his jacket pocket and called the last and only number which had rung it.

"Hello?"

"Good, B. You're doing well. Now, I want you to ride the cable car until you get to Powell, then get out and take the Powell car toward Chinatown."

"But I can get out in Chinatown right at California."

"Please follow my instructions, or I'm out of here."

"Okay, okay." Bryce coughed and held out the phone, then placed it back. "I will, don't worry."

Robert clicked off and walked ahead to the intersection of Powell and California Streets. From his pre-selected vantage point, he watched Bryce's California Street car stop, heard the bells chime, and saw Bryce exit the car along with about six other people. Three of them scattered in different directions and three waited in the street along with Bryce for the Powell Street car.

Robert made a mental note of all three persons and walked down the hill to catch the Powell Street cable car. When it arrived at the California Street intersection, the operator cranked the brake and it came to a halt. Robert watched Bryce get on and take a seat. Two of the three others sat down together and the third one who had been standing with Bryce stood on the running board of the car.

Robert called Bryce and instructed him to exit the car at Washington. Robert exited two streets before, at Sacramento, and walked along, watching the car. One of Bryce's "companions" – the one standing, got off at Clay. Robert watched as the car inched to a stop at Washington and Bryce exited it alone. He rang Bryce once more.

"Throw the phone in the nearest garbage can and walk west on Washington until you get to Columbus. I'll make contact with you there."

Bryce did as instructed, disposing of his phone in a garbage can on Washington. When he reached Columbus, he stopped and looked around nervously. A boy came up to him and tugged on his jacket. Bryce was startled, but looked down at the boy and smiled. "Yes?"

"You're Bryce?"

"Yes."

The kid held out an envelope. "This is for you."

"Thanks," Bryce said, taking the envelope as the boy ran away. He opened it, and read: "Take a left to Yan's Kitchen. Last table on the right."

Robert slipped back into the restaurant as Bryce proceeded, still alone, and still as directed. Robert could hear Bryce sputtering and watched him through the glass storefront as he entered the café and approached the wooden table on the far right. Robert nodded and Bryce sat down on one of the three wooden chairs.

"Pleased to finally meet you." Bryce held out his hand and Robert took it in his, tentatively.

"Sorry for the clandestineness. I had to make sure you weren't being followed. Hey, the dim sum is really good here. You want some?"

"Sure."

Bryce told Robert the story of his son, of Bryce's foundation to fight terrorism and of his personal losing battle with cancer. The story lasted until the last dim sum was consumed.

"So you want this terrorist to disappear?"

"First him, yes. Then I want them *all* to disappear."

Robert ran his hand through his black beard. "I see. Sounds like a full time job. I usually just take one assignment at a time."

"I'll pay you well."

"You'll have to."

Bryce laughed and the laugh turned into a hack. He covered his mouth and swallowed, just as the waiter brought another assortment of dim sum in a woven basket and put it in the middle of the table, along with three kinds of sauce.

"I've got all the information on the first one here." Bryce slid an envelope across the table to Robert. "And there's fifty thousand in cash, small bills, old. Don't worry. I've been saving this cash for a long time."

Robert nodded, but let the envelope lie. "And the next one?"

"One of the perks of being rich is that a bunch of politicians owe me favors. I've got direct access to the FBI's TSDB database."

Robert stabbed at a dim sum with his chopsticks, dipped it in some red sauce and plopped it in his mouth. "This stuff is good, but in my business, I can never stick around long. Enjoy it, B."

Robert stood up and stuffed the packet under his arm.

"I'll be in touch."

Bryce sputtered and said, "Wait, what should I call you?"

"Anything you want." Robert smiled. 'I'm a man of many names." Robert slipped away past the counter and into the kitchen toward the exit.

Bryce nodded and thought, *Paladine.*

CHAPTER NINE

Robert made his way back to the Bradley Hotel, following counter-surveillance moves to make sure he was not being followed or to confuse anyone who was tailing him. He headed up Washington about half a block, then ducked into an alley for a few moments. Then he backtracked the same route, getting lost in the crowd on the street. Robert chose a different route to reach his hotel, which was not far from Union Square. When he was finally in the room, he tore open the envelope.

The bulk of the package consisted of stacks of worn $100 bills, which Robert examined carefully with an ultraviolet light. He noted the serial numbers of the bills as he counted them and they appeared to be random – not sequential – which would have made him suspect this was a set-up. The bills, which totaled $50,000, appeared to be unmarked and useable. Robert would need some of them to prepare for this hit.

The rest of the paperwork consisted of several photographs and a short dossier on the subject. Robert didn't need to do any research on his target. He recognized the man immediately. It was Aaresh Shanahwaz, the Afghani terrorist who had killed Williamson's son in a car attack in 2006. The target was serving an insanity stint at Atascadero State Hospital, which was halfway to Los Angeles. Robert had to take more precautions than usual with this job because of its connection to Bryce Williamson. His son had been the only fatality in the attack and if the hit was connected to Williamson, it would mark the end of Robert's association with him. He decided the best thing to do was to make it look like an accident.

Robert had two impediments to overcome. One, the lethal element he had chosen, potassium chloride, was readily available in pharmaceutical grades from the traditional Internet. Potassium chloride broke down into natural elements in the body, but an overdose of it would stop Shanahwaz's heart like a clock. But Robert could not receive a delivery. Moreover, the second impediment was much worse – Atascadero State Hospital was a high security facility that housed most of the criminally insane who had the unfortunate circumstance of being caught in the California criminal courts system. It was a risky job, but nothing worthwhile was ever accomplished without some kind of a gamble. But, as Robert studied photographs and plans for the institution, he became convinced there was no way he could sneak in and poison his target. He would have to be taken out from afar.

Robert needed mobility but at the same time invisibility. He couldn't rent a car. Besides, cops had a habit of stopping cars, sometimes for no reason. A motorcycle would give him more maneuverability and would be good for quick escapes. He paid cash to a private party for a used Kawasaki KLR650. This bike would be good for street or off-road use. He would keep the pink slip unregistered so it was untraceable and could be abandoned on less than a moment's notice. He picked up some second hand hunting wear and gear at a nearby Army surplus store.

Robert rode down to Atascadero. He found the hospital, which resembled a prison, easily, and stashed the bike in a clump of trees in the mountainous area overlooking the facility. Robert hiked to a reconnaissance point which he had selected with his high-powered binoculars, mainly for its tree cover. Focusing on the center from a distance of about 500 yards, which was as close as he could get and still have the cover of the local brush, he studied the layout of the facility. The hospital had a prison-style observation tower, but instead of one on every corner, there was one in total – a solitary tower that didn't have an accurate perspective for surveillance of the courtyard.

This was going to be a difficult and dangerous job, but Robert relished the challenge. The outdoor areas, separated from the outside by an inner fence, consisted of a courtyard area and baseball diamond. He stayed long enough to see the inmates in the courtyard in the early afternoon. Some were playing cards, some playing ping-pong, but most of them were either standing around smoking or shuffling through the yard in their khaki green scrubs.

Robert studied their faces carefully but did not find the one he was looking for. In a perfect world, he would have liked to do 24-hour surveillance on the hospital for about a week, in order to plot patterns and times, and especially to locate his target, but this was an indulgence he could not afford himself. Robert would have to take the first opportunity that presented itself, strike immediately, and then vanish without leaving a trace behind. Luckily for him, the hospital had been designed to prevent inmates from escaping, not to prevent them from being assassinated.

At dusk, Robert hit the road and headed for Bakersfield. Robert made his way to the part of town filled with cheesy motels and even cheesier hookers, and checked in anonymously to one of the rooms like the dozens of other "John Smiths" that had been coming and going. As he lay in bed, he listened to the unmistakably genuine grunting and groaning and pseudo cries of passion from various rent-a-chicks throughout the night. Robert thought of indulging his own restrained libido, but phantoms don't have sex and Robert could not afford to have a physical presence. Besides, call girls had a reputation for being more selective than motel managers. Years of abuse by johns had taught them to be discreet and to check ID. It was easier to cash a check in Bakersfield than it was to get laid. Robert fell asleep to the resonance of the orgasmic buzz of the animal kingdom wafting through the grounds of the Jacks or Better Motel.

When Robert awoke in the morning, he snuck out as quietly as he had slipped in. He tossed down a morning coffee – black – and a Grand Slam breakfast at a local Denny's and then called a number that he had memorized for many years for tools of the trade shopping. Robert met an anonymous gun dealer in a hotel room outside of town. He selected a Remington 700 .308 rifle with a long-distance scope. He was readily familiar with this particular piece of equipment because it was used by snipers in the US Army. It was also a perfectly legal hunting gun, although Robert did not intend it to be used for legal hunting. He put Bakersfield in his rearview.

CHAPTER TEN

Robert stashed his bike in the woods and hiked the short distance to the vantage point he had selected. He crouched in the shadows of the cluster of trees and bushes and peered through his binoculars above the rifle which had been set up on its bipod and aimed at the courtyard, safety clicked forward, ready to fire, and began the unknown countdown to the kill.

From time to time, Robert looked through the scope and fixed the sight on several landmarks in the courtyard – the ping pong tables and benches used by the inmates of the hospital during their yard time. He had calculated the slight wind resistance and projectile direction and was about 500 yards away from any potential target in the yard – an acceptable distance for the Remington 700. He was not likely to, nor could he afford to miss. Once he had identified the target and confirmed his identity, Robert had a mere few seconds to aim and take his shot, and a window of about sixty seconds before his whereabouts became known within which to bolt and make his getaway. He had planned his escape route carefully.

Robert simulated his shot, relaxed and practiced his breathing protocol, since he would have only seconds to prepare between the time he spotted his target until he had to pull the trigger.

Finally, Robert spotted his prey in a group of inmates coming out onto the yard. Aaresh Shanahwaz appeared to be in a drunken, probably drugged stupor. He shuffled out into the courtyard, took up a lone position leaning against an outer wall, brought a cigarette to his mouth, and lit it. Robert lay down stretched out before his rifle, resting his right cheek against the laminated wood stock, closed his left eye and focused the right one on the target. The optics were so good he could see the beard hairs on Shanahwaz's chin and the perspiration above his brow.

Robert exhaled, his finger gripping the trigger with pinpoint accuracy. In a clean, smooth pull, he fired two successive shots to Shanahwaz's chest, and kept his eye focused through the sight on the target to confirm the hits. The first shot was a direct hit to his core, and brought him down like a duck in a carnival shooting gallery. Seeing him fall, a nurse and attendant ran to Shanahwaz's aid. Robert broke down the rifle, sheathed it in its case, and slipped away. He reached his motorbike within seconds and sped off on State Route 41 toward the Pacific Ocean drop site in Morro Bay, about a fifteen-minute ride, ten if Robert was lucky.

He pulled up to a spectacular rocky ocean cliff, drove the bike as far as he could and then walked to the outermost edge of the rocky ledge that jutted out into the sea. He weighted down the Remington and then tossed it into the churning waters below.

Once they had determined that Shanahwaz had been shot, hospital police officers were crawling all over the perimeter and outskirts of the grounds. By that time, Robert had traveled south through San Luis Obispo, and Pismo Beach.

When the local authorities and the FBI had come on the scene, he was already in Bakersfield.

Robert navigated the spaces between the long line of Friday traffic on its way to Las Vegas, flying between the stop-and-go traffic crawling up the I15. He had selected Sin City as the perfect place to hole up until the situation cooled off. When he finally rolled into town, he picked a Mail Boxes Etc address off the beaten path and signed up for a mailbox. Then, he checked himself into a motel located next door to a restaurant with hackable WiFi and surfed the Net for news. All outlets were reporting the apparent murder of Aaresh Shanahwaz and his only claim to fame: the murderous SUV spree which left dozens injured and one dead in 2006. The dead victim was named as John Williamson. Robert knew that, by this time, the police were all over Bryce Williamson, which meant that this may be the first and last job Robert ever did for his generous employer.

CHAPTER ELEVEN

Bryce Williamson inhaled the mist from the steaming cup of coffee. Even with all the pain and discomfort he could still enjoy this one morning pleasure. He also had the ancient happiness of feeling the newsprint of the San Francisco Chronicle. It had become thinner since the assault waves of the so-called Internet journalism of hack writers and bloggers, which had taken their toll on the news. The front page was particularly satisfying, because the headlines told the story of the demise of the despicable terrorist who had taken the life of his son.

As he raised the fine porcelain cup to his lips to enjoy one of his life's last diversions, the phone buzzed. He picked it up and the receptionist informed him that two gentlemen dressed in polyester suits were waiting in the lobby to speak to him.

"Did they show ID?"

"No, sir."

"Feds," Bryce whispered, under his breath.

"Make them show ID and, if they're from the government, send them in. If they're not, tell them to make an appointment."

Moments later, two suited agents of the Federal Bureau of Investigation were entering Bryce's office. The one leading the charge was short, with an obvious Napoleon complex, and the second one was taller than average. The short one introduced them both with a sneer and an insincere outstretched hand.

"Mr. Williamson, I'm Special Agent Dubrovnik and this is Special Agent McHenry from the FBI." His voice was nasal, like he had something stuffed up his nose.

Bryce remained seated and allowed Dubrovnik's hand to languish in the wind. McHenry toothed a goofy smile. He seemed friendly enough to Bryce. Maybe it was going to be a game of "good cop, bad cop."

"Have a seat, gentlemen, I was just having a cup of coffee. Would you like one?"

Dubrovnik's sneer turned into a frown as he lowered himself onto the velvet cushion of the Louis IV chaise. Both of them answered in the affirmative on the coffee and Bryce pushed the intercom and ordered two more cups sent in. No pot, they wouldn't be staying. McHenry flipped open a steno book and started to write furiously.

"You boys must be busy. What brings you here?"

"You don't know?" Dubrovnik couldn't contain himself. He blurted out the reason for their call before Bryce could ignore the question. "The murder of Aaresh Shanahwaz."

Bryce left Dubrovnik's statement smoldering, without gratifying his interrogator. Finally he responded, "You mean the execution of the terrorist who killed my son? You boys are about…" He checked his Piguet. "…Almost ten years late. But I'm glad someone has finally done your job."

"The court found Mr. Shanahwaz insane. The crime we're investigating is his murder."

"All jihadists are insane, gentlemen. That doesn't mean they shouldn't be executed." Bryce coughed phlegm into his handkerchief.

"You wanted nothing more than Shanahwaz dead, isn't that true?"

Bryce said nothing.

"I take that as an admission," Dubrovnik delightfully declared as McHenry scribbled on his pad, flipping a page and getting right back to it.

"The only admission is the obvious incompetence of your department. Now, please tell me the reason for your visit."

The tall grandson of the Irish immigrants looked up from his notebook to answer. "We'd like to talk about the murder, uhm, what you're calling an execution."

"Then why don't you talk to the executioner?"

The receptionist knocked on the door and excused herself as she placed a silver tray on the desk before the G-Men which contained two saucered porcelain cups and a silver sugar bowl and creamer.

"Thank you, Jessica. Gentlemen, enjoy your coffee and then you're going to have to excuse me. If you wish to speak about this or any other matter, Jessica will give you the name of my lawyer. That's what they're for, you know." Bryce smiled and sipped. Dubrovnik looked like a kid who had had his ice cream cone stolen by a bully. McHenry continued to take notes.

Dubrovnik stood up and McHenry, open mouthed, shut his notebook and also stood, following the example of his leader, who resembled a pouting boy who had been told that his friends didn't want to play with him anymore. Both held out their hands for a shake and a smile, but their false courtesies were not returned.

"I guess there's nothing more to talk about. If you change your mind…"

"I won't."

Dubrovnik reached for his jacket pocket with his useless hand and withdrew a card. As if on cue, McHenry did the same.

"Here are our cards. Give us a call."

"Don't hold your breath, gentlemen. I'm sure you already know that I have stage 4 cancer. Talk to my lawyer if you want. My time is much more valuable than you realize, and you can be thankful not to be in the same position."

"Even cancer patients can go to prison." Dubrovnik snickered, attempting to have the last word. Williamson deprived him of that pleasure.

"So can federal agents." Bryce smiled with satisfaction. "Good day, gentlemen. If you should find yourselves back in this office, please call ahead to make an appointment."

The two exited the office, a boy whose toys had been stolen and his puppy-dog companion.

CHAPTER TWELVE

Robert was not the type who could own or possess anything. Everything was disposable. He rented a storage unit for the 650 from a storage facility where the manager agreed to take dead presidents in place of ID. Robert liked the bike, and he would need transportation, but it would have to stay here and he would use it only for jobs. It could be disposed of at a moment's notice and nobody would ever tie it to him. On the other hand, he also needed to live in the real world and that meant that Julio Ignacio would have to get a place to live and a way to get around. But he couldn't find a residence without a ride. Robert liked the ease of mobility and agility of the motorbike, so he found a good used Honda NC700X from a private party and paid cash. Unlike the KLR, he would have to register this bike.

Robert waited in line patiently at the DMV. He was not sure when he would be able to do another job, but the money left over from the last endeavor would last him a while. He had decided to stay in one place while he spent it, and Las Vegas was as good as any place. It was crowded, transient, and despite the fact that it had more FBI agents and IRS agents than any other city in America, it was somewhere he thought he could hide in plain sight.

When he got his number, he sat down with the clipboard they had given him and filled out his driver's license and registration applications. Then, when his number was called, he went to window number seven, where he found a clerk that proved not to be harmful to his eyes. It had been some time since Robert had really been attracted to somebody.

Virginia Linder smelled like a beautiful country meadow after a fresh spring rain. Her long blonde hair that had been tied in pigtails reminded him of Sabrina Fair, his first love. Her puffy cheeks dimpled when she spoke and he imagined his lips pressed up against hers. Robert stood in front of her, temporarily lost in a fugue state of daydream.

"I said, may I help you, sir?"

"Huh?" Robert flinched, back to reality. "I'm sorry, yes, I'm here to register my vehicle and to apply for a driver's license."

Virginia smiled. "Do you have a driver's license in any other state?"

"No."

"Alright, then, may I please see your application, your proof of birth, ID and proof of Nevada residence?"

Robert dealt over a package of papers and documents, which Virginia flipped through quickly. "Do you have another document to prove your residence, like a utility bill?"

Robert frowned. "No, I just moved here."

Virginia slid the documents back to him. "Well, we'll just need a utility bill. A phone bill or power bill will be fine. Then we can complete both of these applications."

Robert nodded politely, thanked her, and left, with a vision of her beauty etched against his retinas.

***

When Robert arrived home, he flipped open his laptop, checked it for bugs, then, using the WiFi from next door, activated his TOR browser. There was a message waiting for his PGP key: *Work for You.*

At 7 p.m., Robert warily joined *Wild Bill,* aka Bryce Williamson in the encrypted private chat room as he had requested, using the handle, *P:*

I HAVE WORK FOR YOU.

TOO HOT. CAN'T DO IT.

DON'T WORRY. EVERYTHING IS SAFE, WE NEED TO TALK.

NEGATIVE.

ON YOUR TURF AND TERMS.

WILL GET BACK TO YOU. ERASE YOUR HARD DRIVE AND DESTROY YOUR CELL PHONES.

Robert took a blank piece of paper and began to make notes. Another meeting with Bryce would be very dangerous. Because of his relationship to the victim, it was very likely his calls and emails were being monitored. If he was also under physical surveillance, arranging and holding a meeting with him without the feds knowing would be a true test of Robert's capabilities, especially if Bryce was cooperating with them.

CHAPTER THIRTEEN

Robert found himself a nice, long-term rental apartment hotel that suited his needs for the moment. He called the phone company who installed a telephone that he would never use in order to establish his proof of Nevada residence for the DMV, but he linked the account to the mail box address. Robert had used some of his stash to get another passport that he may need for a quick identity change. He spent the evening planning out his meeting with Bryce Williamson.

At mid-day, Robert packed lightly and hit the I15. The sun beat down on his back and the wind pelted bugs against his helmet and goggles for the next eight hours, until he finally parked his bike in a downtown parking area and took the Powell-Hyde cable car to the top of San Francisco's famous Lombard Street, known as the most crooked street in the world. There were so many lookie-loos always driving down the twisty, turny street with its eight hairpin curves that it took about 15 minutes to complete the one- block trip. Robert studied the street with his field binoculars and then took the cable car back down the hill toward Chinatown. He checked into a local Starbucks, bought himself a black coffee and hooked in to the café's free WiFi. Within moments, Robert had sent Bryce an encrypted PGP message, logged off and left the Starbucks.

***

Bryce Williamson checked in with his TOR browser and learned that Paladine had left him a message with his concierge, and that he should retrieve the message in a way that did not deviate from his usual, everyday routine. Bryce had been known to break away from his self-imposed monotony for a drink from time to time, so he dressed for the evening, called for his car, and took the message from the concierge on his way out.

He opened the message in the car, which instructed him to proceed down Lombard Street, then slip out of the car at the last turn, grab a cab on Leavenworth and get out at 3158 Mission. Bryce did as he was instructed, and Robert sat on his motorcycle and watched Bryce's car as it entered the one-way street. About halfway through the fourth hairpin turn, there did not appear to be anyone following Bryce's car, which was a good thing. Robert headed on to the meeting place at El Rio Bar.

El Rio was already popping for the evening, and Robert took a spot in the busy, crowded courtyard and ordered a beer while he listened to live music. A decent-looking twenty-something brunette was writhing around on the dance floor and caught Robert's eye. He watched her as he sipped his brew, all the while thinking that his voyeurism had gone unnoticed. He discovered he was wrong when she bumped up to his table, and pointed to the seat beside him with a feminine snap.

"This seat taken?"

Robert set down his mug. "Yes, it is. I'm waiting for somebody."

"Shame," she said through pouted lips and, without missing a beat, danced on to the next table.

Bryce showed up about 20 minutes later, carrying a brown laptop bag, and found Robert in the midst of what was looking like a popular meat market. He took a seat on the wooden bench opposite him.

"Do you have my note?"

Bryce handed the note to Robert, who held it over the ash tray and burned it with his lighter.

"They're not tailing you, at least not today, but you can't take any chances. And I can't be meeting you like this anymore."

"I know. That's why I'm giving you this." Bryce slid his bag to Robert under the table. "There's an advance in there for ten more jobs. I've also included the access codes for the TSDB database. I don't know how often they change them, so get as much information as you can. You choose the jobs."

This all made sense to Robert. The only glitch was that he did not know if he could trust Bryce. As a general rule, Robert didn't trust anyone, but, given the number of inevitable connections which occurred between people on a daily basis, it was impossible to avoid some kind of social contact, unless of course you lived on Mars.

"I choose the jobs?"

"Yeah." Bryce started sputtering, and pulled out his handkerchief to cover his mouth.

"You don't care which ones I do?"

Bryce folded away his handkerchief. "On the contrary, my dear Paladine, I want you to do *all of them*."

CHAPTER FOURTEEN

Robert left Bryce and the bar tab at the El Rio and began to separate his existence from San Francisco. He stopped in a secure area off the road and opened the case. In it were mostly piles of rubber-banded one-hundred-dollar bills and a small slip of paper with the access codes to the database on it. Robert memorized the codes and transferred the money to his backpack. He dumped the case in a city garbage bin.

On the long ride home, Robert contemplated the propriety of his decision to hang his hat for a while in Las Vegas. He quickly dismissed those thoughts by resolving that he could leave on less than a moment's notice and disappear into the wind if need be. Robert pulled into the Barstow Outlets along the I15, grabbed an In-N-Out cheeseburger and settled at the Starbucks next door to caffeinate himself for the remainder of his journey.

He opened his TOR browser using the free wireless connection and surfed his way through the TSDB database, pretending to be a deputy sheriff. The database had a coding system for classifying suspects, with code 1 being the highest risk and code 4 the lowest. There were 318 names in code 1 and 2, which is where Robert would start. He downloaded the data for the 318 on an external hard drive and ended his trespassing session without leaving a digital fingerprint.

***

The code 1 suspect on the top of the list was Aqwa Bukhari, a Pakastani sheik who was suspected of establishing jihadist training camps in the United States for the organization, *American Muslims*. When the FBI came knocking at their door, they simply hid behind the Second Amendment, which allowed them to train their subjects to fire assault weapons. Robert had an inherent mistrust for the government, so he decided to do his own investigation. He hit the traditional Internet and uncovered reports on the organization and their training camps, including their headquarters in New York. The Colorado camp of their suspected parent organization in Pakistan, which was classified a terrorist organization, had been raided by federal agents, who had found explosives, weapons and evidence of terrorism plots and financing, but were prevented from prosecuting because the group hid behind the First and Second Amendments. They had freedom of expression and religion as well as the right to bear arms. The camps would be a great place to work on, but Robert would need a team for that, which meant disclosure. The more people who knew about him, the more risk he would expose himself to, no matter how much he trusted the members of the team.

Robert decided to cut the head off the snake. Taking out Bukhari would be a lot easier than taking out a camp of jihadists and terrorists in training with automatic weapons. With a few more passes over the keyboard, which included a visit to the American Muslim's website, which promoted peace, harmony and tolerance, he discovered that Bukhari would be making a speech at the Colorado complex in two weeks. He made a mental list of the supplies he would need as well as a note in his cerebral calendar.

**

Robert cleared his browsing history, powered off his computer, gathered his dossier for the DMV and tucked it into his bag. When he opened the door to leave, he almost tripped over a dirty, skinny, pitiful looking dog that was sitting on his welcome mat. The mutt had a lamentable, long sad, fuzzy muzzle, and he was staring directly at Robert with his big eyes.

"Get out of here!"

The dog hung his head low and his droopy ears fell even lower.

"I said get out!"

The canine put his head on the deck and covered it with his paws. Robert laughed.

"Okay, okay, I guess that's worth something. You're hungry, right?"

The dog came to attention, his tongue hanging out and eyes wide open as Robert turned to go back in. The dog tentatively put one paw inside the door. Robert instinctively sensed the invasion and turned on him.

"Out! I didn't say you could come in!"

The dog quickly withdrew, hanging back and wagging his long tail enthusiastically. Robert looked through his kitchen for any leftovers he could find. Some of them, like the uneaten fajitas and moldy cheese, probably should be thrown out, but he was sure the dog could handle them. He laid out the barely edible treasures on a piece of wax paper and brought them to the dog, whose tail wagged even more furiously as he patiently waited for Robert to set down the goodies.

As the dog scarfed down the leftover garbage from Robert's fridge, Robert scavenged for a pail, filled it with water, and put it outside the door. The dog quickly stuck his head into the bucket and feverishly lapped up half the contents.

"Slow down, now."

The dog lifted his dripping face and looked up at Robert thankfully.

"Now when I get back, I expect you to be gone."

The dog just wagged his tail as Robert shut and locked the door and walked away. The manager's door cracked open after Robert had passed. Robert whirled around.

"You want something?"

Caught with his pants down, the manager scratched his 9 am shadow and pulled his used to be white T-shirt down over his ample beer belly. "It's just that I didn't know you had a dog."

"I don't have a dog."

"Well I saw one up at your apartment."

Robert mentally counted to ten. This guy really needed a punch in the nose, but he wasn't going to be the designated puncher. "I told you, Billy, it's not my dog."

Billy scratched his nose. "Cuz, if you had a dog, we'd have to charge an extra security deposit."

Robert said nothing, just stared right at Billy's nose, an intent and fixed stare. "Okay, okay, if he's not yours, then, I guess we've got no issues."

"Good."

Robert didn't need any issues. Or a dog.

CHAPTER FIFTEEN

Robert traded his number several times, allowing people to go ahead of him at the DMV. He wanted Virginia's window, not because he was smitten with her, but because she knew his case and he wouldn't have to explain everything all over again. She greeted him with a wide smile.

"You're back."

Robert looked down. "Yep."

"Got everything this time?"

Robert nodded and put his papers on the counter. She took them and riffled though them.

"Uh-oh." She was looking in the papers. What could she possibly need now?

Virginia lifted her head, smiling again. "Just kidding! Everything's here."

She processed his paperwork, gave him his Nevada plates, and directed him to the driver's license test.

"When you get done, don't wait in line, just come back to my window."

"Thank you, Virginia."

She looked startled, then tapped her name tag and smiled. That smile turned out to be contagious.

***

On the floor of the National Counterterrorism Center, which looked like NASA's Mission Control with its massive viewing screens and rows and rows of computers with scores of analysts sitting in front of them, Nathan Anderson directed the action on the big screens.

"What have you got on the jihadist nut-job who got snuffed out in the looney bin in California?" Anderson directed his comment to the "Clark Kent" type at the desk directly in front of the largest screen.

"We figure it was a hit put out by one of the victim's fathers. Name's Bryce Williamson. Just established a foundation against terrorism in his son's name."

"Have you got the feed from the surveillance cameras outside his house?"

The big screen came to life, showing the street outside Williamson's building. "No unusual comings or goings, no different visitors, either before or after the hit."

"The FBI talk to him?"

"Yes, they've got nothing. Apparently the guy has stage four cancer and hasn't got long to live."

"So he's cleaning house."

"Apparently so."

"Well, keep an eye on him, Jack, in case he decides to take any more jihadists to Nirvana with him."

"Yes, sir."

Anderson wasn't worried about the last wish avengement of an old man dying of cancer. He wanted Paladine.

***

Reclining in his soft leather chair, Bryce Williamson flipped his TV remote, covering the basic news channels. Although there had been a terrorist attack in Europe and the usual suicide bombings in the Middle East, there was nothing on any new jihadist assassinations. It was exasperating for him not to contact Paladine, but he had given him carte blanche to select and execute his own jobs, so he turned to the business of the foundation, which was about to walk into his office.

The receptionist announced Elizabeth Rubinstein, a career senator from California who had been in office ever since her first wrinkle. The senator seemed to drift into the office on her own air, which was fine with Bryce. He could understand ego. After all, he had helped build it with his generous contributions to every one of her campaigns from Day One. It was payback time, but it was the kind of recompense that would sit well with the senator, who was a staunch proponent of gun control.

Bryce stood and their outstretched hands met in the middle.

"So good of you to come, senator. Please, sit down."

"It was my pleasure. When I heard you were ill, I knew I had to spare you the trip."

Bryce held his hand to his mouth as he coughed and nodded. "Thank you. Excuse me, senator." She waved it off and smiled.

"My foundation for counterterrorism has hired the best legislation lawyers in the country. I have here," he said, patting his hand on a ream of paper, "the most important bill you perhaps will ever have the pleasure of reviewing. I would be most proud if you could bring yourself to sponsor it."

"Well, of course I'll have to read it first."

"Of course," said Bryce, knowing she never would. A staffer in her office would read it and give her a report of the highlights. "Simply put, if a person has been placed on the terrorism watch list, he or she cannot pass the screening to buy any kind of a weapon."

Rubinstein's eyebrows raised.

"Of course, there is an appeal process. We've thought of every nuance." He slid the mass of paper across the desk to her. "The DVD with the entire bill is in the envelope. You will let me know if you're interested?"

"Of course. I hear your foundation is doing some wonderful things to insure that terrorism is wiped off the planet."

Bryce nodded and smiled. *You don't know the half of it.*

CHAPTER SIXTEEN

Robert returned home to find that mangy mutt curled up on his welcome mat.

"Hey, scram!"

The dog just wagged his tail. Robert stepped over him, went in and slammed the door. With second thoughts, he opened it again and the pitiful creature looked up at him with his big, hopeful eyes.

"Water and whatever I can find in the fridge, then you beat it!" He grabbed the water bucket, slammed the door again, then returned with a fresh water and some leftover steak, which the dog scarfed down in seconds.

Robert went back inside, booted up his laptop and continued his faux jihadist quest in the sewers of the Darknet's virtual caliphate. Robert's research had shown him that the jihadist movement was mostly young people, and most of them were not from the Middle East. They had rejected the establishment's teachings of moderate Islam. It was a youth revolt against society whose members were from the late teens into their early twenties. He made several "friends" including one who claimed he had been chosen for martyrdom, and who furiously chatted about his plans.

I HAVE BEEN CHOSEN BY THE DAESH TO BE A SHAHID AND DO MY PART IN THE HOLY WAR AGAINST THE APOSTATES.

I HEAR YOU, BROTHER. SALAM ALEIKOM.

AND WITH YOU, BROTHER. ALLAHU AKBAR.

ALLAHU AKBAR. HOW WILL YOU ACCOMPLISH THIS HONOR, BROTHER?

THEIR EVIL, BLASPHEMIC MUSIC. IT IS HARAM! I WILL SNUFF IT OUT IN THE NAME OF ALLAH! THEY BLASPHEME THE PROPHET MOHAMMAD!

Robert could sense his excitement. So, the hit was most likely to occur at a concert or some venue where music was playing. That, most likely, meant an explosive device.

SURELY, BROTHER, YOU CANNOT DO THIS ALONE.

WITH ALLAH, WE ARE NEVER ALONE.

Sounds like a loner.

TRUE, BUT LIKE YOU, I ALSO FEEL MY DESTINY IN MARTYRDOM. THIS SOUNDS LIKE A VERY WORTHY CAUSE.

DAESH SAYS THAT KILLING EVEN ONE INFIDEL IS ENOUGH, BUT I PLAN TO KILL HUNDREDS, MAYBE EVEN THOUSANDS.

IT DEPENDS ON WHAT YOU USE, WHETHER IT'S AN IED OR VEST.

No answer. It could be either.

WHAT IS YOUR NAME, BROTHER?

IT WILL BE WRITTEN IN THE BROTHERHOOD OF THE PROTECTORS OF MUSLIM UMMAH.

The screen went blank. *He said they blaspheme Mohammad.* Robert's hands flew across the keyboard. The search results popped up right away.

Here it is. Black metal band, whose anti-Islamic lyrics damn Mohammad – Temke – and they have a concert in Phoenix on Friday.

The venue for the concert was Club Fed, a strange name for a heavy metal venue, but good for Robert because it was not a huge stadium and there was only one main entrance for patrons.

Robert's call to action could not wait for Aqwa Bukhari's speech. This was a chance for Paladine to really put his calling card out there and diversify – less risk with multiple employers. He had to get to Phoenix, and right away.

CHAPTER SEVENTEEN

Robert didn't know what he would be facing in Phoenix, so he called a number that he had filed in his head, met with a private gun dealer and picked himself up another Remington 700 with opticals. Since it didn't pack well on a motorcycle, Robert also visited a local music shop and bought a guitar with case. Maybe he would take up the guitar sometime, but for now he kept it in his apartment. The case was for the gun.

The packing finished, Robert headed out the door – a music groupie on his way to a heavy metal concert - and almost tripped over the dog. The dog shot up and instantly started wagging his tail.

"I thought I told you to get lost!"

The dog hung his pitiful, droopy head.

Robert shook his head. He went back in the apartment, filled up the water bucket to the top, put almost all the contents of his refrigerator on a baking tray, and set it out in front for the dog. When Robert tried to leave again, the pesky manager got in his face.

"I thought you said you didn't have a dog."

"I don't," said Robert, slipping on his dark glasses.

"What's that?" The manager nudged his head toward the dog.

"It's not mine. I'll figure out what to do with him when I come back."

"I can call the pound and they'll pick him up."

"Don't they kill them in there?"

"Well, yeah, if nobody claims 'em."

"Nobody's gonna claim this dirty ole mutt." Robert looked down at the dog, who responded with a tail wag, his tongue hanging out and panting. Robert shook his head.

"Well, then I guess I'll call 'em."

Robert took off his glasses and leaned penchant within an inch of the man's face, staring at him with firm but emotionless expression. "I don't think that's a good idea for you. Why don't you just wait until I get back?"

The manager backed off. "Okay, whatever you say." Robert gave him the creeps sometimes.

Robert flipped his shades back on and headed for his motorcycle. The plan was still incomplete. Maybe it would come together on the ride.

***

When Robert got to Phoenix, he checked into a cheap motel and went to Club Fed for a bite to eat and a brew. The venue gave away its genre right away – it had a heavy metal dungeon theme, equipped with bars, chains, and of course, skulls. Posters and clothing for heavy metal bands adorned the walls of the bar, including sweat rags and ripped T-shirts thrown off the stage by famous black metal bands such as Immortal, Mayhem, and Slayer.

Robert sat at a corner table and scoped the layout – especially the emergency exits. Security would be heavy, so perhaps the best time to take the hit would be when the jihadist was entering. The only problem was that Robert didn't know what he looked like. He would have to guess. Robert suspected that it would be almost impossible for the asshole to get into the bar with a bomb in his possession or a suicide jacket on, so he would probably choose to detonate it outside when the mass of people waiting was the largest. He would check out any suspicious vehicles within range of the bar. He would also look for a loner – an Arab immigrant or Arab-American, who was nervous and looked out of place, with a bulky jacket to hide his deadly payload.

As Robert left the bar, it was still light outside. He examined the exterior. It was a strip mall with a convenience store, a flower store, a dog groomer. Thanks to the downturn in the economy, there was a vacant store across the parking lot from Club Fed. Its store front windows had been whitewashed. This could provide the perfect cover for Robert to observe the front of the club. He grabbed some food and water from the mini-mart. The next day was going to be a long one.

***

At about 5:30 a.m., Robert picked the lock of the abandoned store in seconds and was in. He took up residence in the back office, which still had an old desk. Robert fired up his "throwaway" laptop, which he used for traveling, as it contained no hard drive and left no digital footprint behind. He hacked into the wireless system of the next door material

73

and pattern store and opened his Onion router in an attempt to get in touch with "Mr. Jihadi."

Surfing the chat rooms he came across several who appeared to be recruiting for ISIS, but no suicide bombers. In fact, he couldn't find any evidence of any type of a planned hit. The guy was obviously one of those home-grown terrorists who planned on doing his own thing and ISIS or Al-Qaeda would take the credit for it after the fact, claim he was a soldier, and had gone to rest in paradise with 72 virgins. Robert had had a virgin once and didn't see the attraction in it. For him it was an unmemorable experience. It was much better to have an experienced woman who knew what she was doing, preferably a pro.

Robert scratched a hole in the whitewashed window which was big enough to look out but small enough for him to retain his invisibility. He spent the hours going back and forth from the office to look for clues for the evening's suicide bombing and the front to check out the preparations for the concert. Finally, about an hour before the doors were to open, he hit virtual pay dirt.

In the chat room where Robert had talked to the young jihadist bomber, there was a link to a video. It looked like it had been filmed in a bedroom in some suburban community with a makeshift ISIS flag in the background. In it, a nervous, bearded, dark skinned young man recited:

In the name of God, the most gracious, the most merciful. Let those who fight in the way of Allah who sell the life of this world for the other. Whoso fight in the way of Allah, be he slain or be he victorious, on him we shall bestow a vast reward. I am a holy soldier. I fight for Allah and on behalf of the Daesh. This is not suicide, it is martyrdom. This is what our enemies fear. It is an obligation for all and those who do not fulfill this obligation are sinners. I invite all my brothers to also sacrifice themselves in order to rid the world of the filthy apostates. Allahu Akbar!

Robert played the video again and again, pausing it to memorize every detail of the face of his target. This little fuck was going to die tonight alright, but he was going to be the only one. Robert was on the hunt again.

CHAPTER EIGHTEEN

For Robert, watching the metalheads line up for Club Fed was like watching a freak show, starring a bunch of long-haired, dreadlocked, shaved-headed and bearded hippie-types with black band shirts covered in black leather. To blend, Robert had a black jacket for the occasion, hair shaved close to the cranium, and he always had a beard. He also dressed his Ruger SR22 with a Silent SR noise suppressor. This hit would be up-close and personal. He suspected that the party-pooper, Mr. Jihadi, would show up at the murder scene not dressed to kill like the others. That would be haram. But he examined all the faces just the same.

Robert could not take the chance of going out into the crowd yet. He had to see his target first. In the excitement and commotion of the melee that was to follow it was not likely anyone would remember his face – only another bearded metal freak in black leather and biker boots.

The chicks were animated, swishing about in their leather lace and spikes and making faces through trashy makeup, while the guys mulled around them, trying to act cool. When the sound of the opening act tuning up reverberated from the bar inside, they flashed "horns" signs and whistled and screamed. Robert watched the line like a chessboard. He would have only one move to make and the timing of it was critical. Straight to checkmate, no time for check.

Suddenly, Robert noticed someone who looked out of place approaching from the left. He had the beard, but none of the dark metal accoutrements. He was a little pudgy, but it was bulk under his jacket rather than a belt line of belly fat that gave him away. He was jittery, looking kind of like a bather on a beach who had water up to his knees but was avoiding that final plunge into the ocean. Robert was 90% sure he had his man, but couldn't see his face for confirmation. He pressed his binoculars to his eyes and waited for the visage to come into focus.

It's him!

Robert's heart was pounding with stone-cold precision. He pulled his ski mask over his head, slipped out of the vacant store and walked straight to the jihadist, as close as he could, leveled his gun and fired three shots to his head and throat. In the split second the man went down Robert vanished like a shadow eclipsed by the moon. People next to the fallen terrorist screamed with confusion. A beef-necked security guard ran to the body and turned it over. Mr. Jihad's neck and chest were covered with blood. The crowd panicked, but instead of dispersing, they came closer to the fallen terrorist, closing in the circle with curiosity. The beef-neck yelled out.

"Get back! This guy's been hurt! Is there a doctor here? Call 9-1-1!"

Another security guard came running, yelling into his walkie-talkie, and noticed something sticking out of the jihadist's jacket near the bottom of the zipper.

"He's got a bomb!"

The masses attempted to scatter in every direction. In their panic, they bumped into each other and knocked each other over. The guards abandoned their posts. The manager came out of the bar yelling, "What's going on out here?"

"This guy's been shot! He's got a bomb!"

By the time the police arrived, there were only a few brave witnesses who had stayed behind for curiosity. The bomb squad disarmed the dead jihadist, clearing the way for Detective Joshua Maynard to try to figure out just what had happened.

Even in his police uniform, Maynard looked more like a cowboy than a homicide detective, as he moseyed through the leftover metalheads, taking statements.

"I saw who did it, man!"

Maynard motioned to the skinny white kid with dreadlocks to come over.

"Who did it?"

"It was Paladine, man."

Maynard had heard of Paladine, but he had written it off to urban legend. Now the bullshit had crept its way into his bailiwick and it gave him pause for thought. It was obviously a professional hit. Someone knew where the bad guy was going to be. But who? And how?

"Can you describe this guy you saw?"

"Dude, he was big. About seven feet tall. And he had a beard."

"What color hair?"

"I dunno. He was wearing a mask."

"White, black?"

"Kinda in-between, you know? I couldn't tell if he was white, black or brown, man. And the weirdest thing was…" The kid drew a blank stare.

"What?"

"He just disappeared into thin air. Like a ghost. That's how come I know it had to be Paladine."

CHAPTER NINETEEN

Nathan Anderson got the alert a split second before it began appearing on computer monitors and television screens. The hashtag #Paladine was trending on Twitter, with scores of stories and even illustrations of what the alleged super hero might look like. ISIS was claiming their downed "soldier" and vowing revenge against all infidels.

Paladine posed a unique dilemma for Anderson. He was a problem, not because he was cleaning up the backyard sleeper cells, but because he was doing it without authority. It was the CIA who sent out assassins, and usually not in their own country. He wondered where this Paladine was getting his intel, and the first answer that was brought to mind made him sick at his stomach – *from us! He's getting it from us!*

Anderson frankly thought that the NCTC could use an army of Paladines, but there was no authority for it in the law. If only they could just tick off the number ones, twos and threes on the watch list with a red check mark that stood for "dead terrorist" without having to mess with gathering evidence, courts and such. After all, we were at war, and like in any war, the rules had to be relaxed for the better good.

But he'd be damned if he'd let a vigilante run around out there claiming all the credit and making them look stupid.

This Paladine was a professional, for sure. But was he an agency man? A retired employee from the company, or even worse, an agent gone rogue? Anderson got on a secure line to the head of the CIA. If this was the agency, then he sure as hell had better know about it.

***

As Robert sped away on his motorbike, he mentally moved $50,000 into the asset column on his balance sheet. Once the road turned into a monotonous and lifeless darkness, he pulled off the highway, onto a dirt road, and off into the desert. He stopped the cycle, withdrew the Ruger and wiped it clean. Then he dug an ample hole and buried it along with its silencer.

Robert mounted the bike and rode back to the highway. The mission was over and done. He had done a good job, but the adrenaline was building up in his head like a pressure cooker. He clamped down on the throttle and opened up the KLR650 to 100 miles per hour.

Robert was famished. His stomach was growling so loud it threatened to overpower the roar of the motor. He pulled over at an Outback Steakhouse in Kingman. He dismounted the bike, walked his rubber legs into the restaurant, and ordered a large bone-in rib eye medium rare. Robert feasted on the bloody meat like the carnivore he was. He pushed the plate away and waved for the waitress who asked if he needed anything else. Robert looked at the steak bone and said, "Yeah, could you please box this up for me?" He walked away from the meal with the bag tucked under his arm, sated and ready to complete the road trip.

When he got home, the dog had disappeared from his front porch, which was all the same to Robert. He chucked the doggy bag from Outback into the trash and forgot about the mangy mutt. But Robert was still pent up and not ready to sleep. He went out and took a membership at 24 Hour Fitness and went through a full routine of pull-ups, lifts and squats. Finally, the pent-up hormones in his blood had settled down and he went home. Robert took a quick shower and turned in. He fell asleep as soon as his head hit the pillow and lasted through the night without dreaming.

***

While Robert was in the sweet stages of slumber, the online world that never slept was conjuring up their versions of Paladine. He was a benevolent do-gooder, a super hero, an assassin, a government-created cyborg. The sketch of the police artist in Phoenix was copied from news report to news report, and went viral on social media. The "eyewitness" account videos by the metalheads on the scene painted the picture of a bigger-than-life paladin, a superman who waged a one-man war against terrorism. He was Jason Bourne, Batman without the costume.

When Robert woke up and swept the Net, he was overwhelmed with images and stories of valor of this non-existent Paladine. He chuckled to himself and shrugged it off. The Internet was a crazy place, especially for what they called "the news." Almost none of it could be believed, so he didn't. For Robert, the truth lay in the balance between life and death. He could feel the rise and fall of his chest and the thumping of his heart. Someday he wouldn't. That was all that there was. No Nirvanah, no greener pastures, no god, just the here and the now. Life today, death tomorrow. He decided to throw a little fuel on the fire, and do some free marketing by hacking into a jihadist's Twitter account and claiming responsibility for the hit as Paladine, making the hashtagged entry go viral.

After Robert left his apartment, he rapped on the manager's door. The manager looked through the peep hole, grimaced, then opened the door.

"Good morning."

"Yeah, whatever, hey, did you see what happened to that dog?"

The manager's brows furrowed. "Dog? Oh, yeah, the dog catcher took him away yesterday."

Robert fixed his eyes on the little ant-man. "I thought I told you not to call them."

The manager practically kneeled in front of him. "I didn't call them, man, I swear. They just came!"

"And you did nothing?"

"What could I do, man?"

Robert turned his back on the squid and headed for his bike. He clenched his fists in anger. He rode to the gym and went inside for another intensive routine. Robert changed into his shorts and tank top. In the free weight room, he loaded four fifty-pounders on the barbell, lay down on the bench and did 50. Then he did sets of alternating deadlifts and squats. Robert was building up a good sweat when he felt that someone was watching him. He used his peripheral vision as he was squatting and spotted her – Virginia from the DMV. When his eyes met hers, she instantly averted them. Robert walked over to her, smiling.

"I didn't know it was your day off."

She regarded him in a strange way, trying to keep her eyes off his massive biceps and shoulders.

"It's Saturday."

"Oh, yeah." Robert felt stupid. In the rush of adrenaline and the expenditures that followed it, he had lost track of time and space. "Well, have a good workout."

"You, too."

Robert waved, turned and started to walk away.

"Hey!" She called out and he pivoted. "You want to grab a bite sometime?"

Robert looked at her, curiously. "A bite?" He approached her again.

"Are those real?" She grazed his biceps with her finger and her touch burned him with pleasure.

"Yep." He flexed it and she covered her mouth with embarrassment. "What were you saying about a bite?"

"You know, a bite. Don't you get hungry?"

Robert took the question literally. "Well, yeah, I get hungry."

She laughed and Robert laughed contagiously. "How about lunch?"

Another thing Robert could not afford was ties. No dogs, no girls. But a little sexual recreation would be nice. Maybe Virginia, despite her name, would make a good fuck buddy.

CHAPTER TWENTY

Bryce Williamson was a dying man, but he was getting his last wish. He knew that the rumors of Paladine striking again meant that Robert was on the job. As he was watching the videos of "eye-witnesses" on TV describing their version of the super hero whom he knew to be no more than a super-assassin, he began to laugh. He stopped laughing when he had coughed up a good amount of blood in his hanky, another reminder that his days, and perhaps even his hours, were limited. It was time to automate the Paladine operation.

Bryce called his attorney and instructed him to draft a codicil to his will, which included a testamentary trust that would survive his death. The trust, among other things, established "The Paladine Foundation" and set up an e-wallet account into which Bitcoins would be deposited on a quarterly basis. It named the current beneficiary of the foundation as "Paladine" and designated him to appoint his own successor. If he failed to do so, the corpus of the trust would revert back to Williamson's estate. It was the only way that Bryce could achieve immortality.

Bryce's mortality came to call that evening when he was rushed to the emergency hospital. The doctors confronted him with the reality he had already known – there was nothing more they could do except keep him comfortable and relatively free of pain. He refused admission to long-term care, instead opting to go home with a full time nurse on duty. Before he was released, he received a visit from a woman with blank eyes, like Robert's. She had grey hair and feigned a kind expression, but Robert could not escape the impression that she looked like a witch. She came at him with her nose like the Wicked Queen in Snow White offering the poison apple.

"Mr. Williamson, I'm Margaret Jordan from San Francisco Hospice Services. I wonder if I may have a few moments of your time?"

Bryce waved her away, but she sat down next to his bed. "No thank you, I don't need you people to help me die. I can do that all by myself."

Jordan smiled. "Mr. Williamson, we're only here to help you. It's you who determines what level of hospice care to receive. I understand that you've opted to have home care."

"Look, lady, I've got everything I need. I can die by myself. I don't need anyone speeding it up or keeping me from enjoying it."

She placed a brochure on his bedside table. "I understand, Mr. Williamson. I'm leaving you some information. In case you change your mind, you can reach me anytime at the number in the pamphlet."

Bryce nodded, "I won't," and the lady bid him farewell and left. He shuddered. *They're not making a zombie out of me. Too much left to do.*

* * *

Nathan Anderson's conversation with Bill Carpenter at the FBI was even less productive than the one he had had with the CIA head, who, of course, knew nothing. Carpenter responded to Anderson in a condescending tone.

"Nathan, aren't you reading a little too much into this *Paladine* thing? It's just a legend, made up by a bunch of kooks on the Internet."

Anderson clutched the phone in frustration. "I think it's more organized than you think, Bill. Plus it's making us look bad. You don't want another Orlando, do you?" Anderson jabbed Carpenter about the FBI's dismal failure to prevent the largest mass shooting in US history when two separate bureau investigations had classified the perpetrator, Omar Mateeen, as no threat.

Carpenter cleared his throat. "You're right about public opinion. I'll form a task force of special agents to look into it."

"I'm not sure if that will be good enough, Bill. Can you assign some agents to work under my supervision? That way, they won't be a chain of command away from the freshest data we have on Paladine."

There was a pause of uncomfortable silence. "I don't know, Nathan. I don't think we really have the authority to do that."

Bullshit.

"Sure you do, Bill, you're the head of the FBI, for Christ's sake."

89

"We'll form the task force, Nathan. Don't worry, I'll get on this personally."

Right.

Nathan hung up the phone more exasperated than he was before the call. Forming a task force was just great. Carpenter would delegate to the head of the task force, then kick back and read (or not read) the reports generated by his agents. What they needed was a concerted effort to catch this guy and whoever was funding him. NCTC's database on potential terrorists was the best in the world, but nobody was using it properly. It was a bunch of different agencies running around like the Keystone Cops, unable to accomplish anything but small-time collars. The government had Abu Bakr al-Baghdadi in custody in 2004 in Iraq and let him go. He then went on to become the caliph of the Islamic State. A major screw-up like that was not going to happen on his watch. It was time to call in the big guns.

Nathan Anderson reported directly to the president of the United States. So, when it came time to make his daily briefing, he decided to give it the personal touch instead of the usual written report. There was an upcoming presidential meeting on national security and, if he had his way, it would be held right there at the NCTC. It was time to give the agency the testosterone it needed and to stop treating Nathan himself like a eunuch. He picked up the secure line and placed a call directly to the Oval Office.

"Nathan, good afternoon, what can I do for you?"

The president was a likeable fellow, always made Nathan feel important and needed, no matter how his hands were tied by legislation or roadblocks in the Congress. Nathan liked him even though he had made the mistake of calling ISIS the "Jaycee team" and thinking about them as such.

"I'm good, Mr. President. Thank you for taking my call."

"Nathan, I talked to Bill Carpenter and I know you're concerned about this *Paladine* thing. Seems to me it's a fictitious character made up to explain some unconnected incidents. I understand you've asked Bill to form a task force. Don't you think that's good enough for now?"

"I'm not so sure they're unconnected, sir, but Paladine wasn't what I wanted to talk to you about."

"Okay, shoot, I'm all ears."

The president had a great sense of humor, better than many stand-up comics, but Nathan was sure that his use of "shoot" and "I'm all ears" was not meant to be funny, even though Paladine was a shooter and the president had a prominent set of Alfred E. Newman ears.

"I'm concerned that this agency has the best tools on this earth to fight terrorism, yet we're failing abysmally in that regard."

"How so? Are you talking about Orlando? I've talked to Bill about that."

"Not just Orlando, Mr. President. This Congressional Report about our shortcomings in the fight against terrorism has been on my desk since 2011."

"I remember it."

"It's a terrible reminder of just how uncoordinated the fight against terrorism is right now between agencies. The report points out that there's a 'wall' between analysts and operators, and the most important part of the fight against terrorism is to make sure that operational planning of enforcement is shared with analytical offices so threats can be adequately anticipated and assessed. With these home-grown terrorists like the one in Orlando becoming more prevalent, I think it's more important than ever to give NCTC a bigger role in the enforcement effort."

"Point taken, Nathan, but what are you suggesting? I don't have to tell you how difficult it would be to get more enabling legislation or funding for your agency, especially now with only two years to go. That bunch wants to put me out to pasture as a lame duck."

"Yes, Mr. President, but I think we already have the necessary framework without having to go back to Congress, which is why I think you should hold your security briefing right here, at NCTC. Let's get everyone together and make a coordinated effort."

There was a pause and the president cleared his throat. "I'll take that under advisement, Nathan, thank you."

With the president and heads of all national security agencies present, Nathan would attempt to make the biggest bureaucratic power grab in his agency's history.

CHAPTER TWENTY ONE

Detective Joshua Maynard scratched his head and rubbed his eyes. The autopsy report didn't give him any more information than he already knew from looking at the body himself. Muhammad Abdul Kareem had been shot at close range with a .22 caliber weapon; a fatal shot to the head, another head shot and a shot to the throat which destroyed a carotid artery. Either one of the other shots would have killed him if the first one hadn't. It had all the marks of a professional hit, including the fact that there was no physical evidence of a murder weapon found on the scene and no decent description of the shooter.

The explanations of witnesses supported the *Paladine* legend, which Maynard knew was a bunch of horse shit, and which had now been turned into a cancer by social media and the mainstream as well. He wondered who could be funding this hitman and where he came from. He deliberated whether there could be any connection between the McDonald's shooting in New York and this case, despite the mythological explanations circulating on the Internet. It looked an awful lot like CIA. If it was, they were way out of line as they had no authority to operate on US soil. Maynard called the investigators in New York who agreed to a mutual exchange of investigation information. He was like a bloodhound. Once he got a sniff of the evidence, whatever that was, he would track it down wherever it led him.

***

With his reading glasses on and staring at his computer screen, Robert Garcia looked more like an analyst or an accountant than an assassin. He studied the framework of Aqwa Bukhari's organization. They knew the outer limits of what was legal and had played it well for years. There was a far-right Christian group that claimed the "American Muslims" organization had established terrorist training camps in their respective settlements. The feds had written the camps off as conspiracy theory, but a raid by Colorado Springs police on a storage locker maintained by Al-Benwa, a terrorist organization founded by Bukhari in Pakistan, had produced firearms, grenades, plastic explosives and target practice silhouettes labeled "Zionist Pig," and "FBI-Anti-Terrorist Team."

The chat rooms and propaganda pages boasted Bukhari would be present for a speech at an alleged terrorist training camp outside Colorado Springs. Robert retrieved satellite and drone images of the compound from the federal government's database, as well as building plans. He chatted with jihadists who planned to travel there to listen to Bukhari speak. This would be Paladine's next operation.

***

Robert had dressed in his best jeans and collared shirt for his lunch date with Virginia. She had offered to meet him at Carson Kitchen, but he wouldn't have it. He told her that a gentleman picks up a lady for a date, and she didn't have any problem with her ride being a motorbike, so Robert met Virginia at her apartment. His nerves were a little shaky when he knocked at her door. It had been a long time. Virginia answered the door smiling.

"Hello, Julio!"

Robert almost looked around to see who she was greeting, but then remembered that was his official name – it's just that nobody had ever called him by it before.

"Hello, Virginia, shall we?" He offered her his arm, she took it, exited and closed and locked her door. Robert walked her to the parking lot to his bike. He detached the extra helmet and held it out to her as he fastened his own. She strapped on the helmet and Robert hoisted her onto the back of the bike, which made her giggle a bit. He took his seat and fired up the motorcycle. Virginia put her hands around Robert's waist. Her touch was firm but gentle and it felt good as Robert took off. It was not something he should get used to.

***

The rooftop patio of the Carson Kitchen downtown was a cool spot with a great view of Las Vegas. Robert and Virginia enjoyed a tray of gourmet cheeseburgers and small talk. Robert thought she was attractive. She had soft, brown hair, a nice, pleasant smile, luscious lips and wide brown eyes. He focused on her ears and thought how he would like to nibble on them, while he was in the process of moving south, of course. Robert already knew what Virginia did for a living, so after she covered her family history (divorced, no kids, one sister and both parents living) she naturally turned the inquiries into his life, which kicked in a playback of Robert's canned stories about his fictitious background, which had been memorized and instilled into his brain as if he could recall them as real memories.

"So what is it that you do, Julio?" She sipped on the straw protruding from a pink concoction which was touted as one of Carson's innovative cocktails. Robert fidgeted. He knew his phony background by heart and could rattle it out on cue, but it had been a long time since he had talked to anyone. People talked about what they knew and about all he knew how to do well was killing people.

"Um, I'm self-employed, pretty much doing odd jobs."

"What kind of odd jobs?"

"Mostly waste management. On a project by project basis."

Virginia nodded without really understanding what he had meant.

"Do you have any family?"

"Nope. Mom and dad are both gone. Never been married. I've got a dog, though."

Virginia's eyes perked up. "A dog? What kind?"

"Oh, you know those Heinz 57 dogs. He's one o' them."

"What's his name?"

Robert paused as he thought, scratched his chin through his beard. "Butthead."

Virginia laughed. It was not a surprise to her that a bachelor had named his dog "Butthead."

"You'll forgive me if I ask how he got that name?"

Robert made a face. "Well, it's actually the first name he responded to."

"That's funny. I'd like to meet your dog. Maybe you could bring him over to my place. I'll make you a nice home cooked meal and he can feast on the leftovers."

"You wouldn't mind having a dog in your house?"

"Why not? I love dogs. Why don't you come on over tomorrow night? Do you like steak?"

"Love it."

"Great."

Once again, the dog had come to Robert's aid, helping him avoid areas of discussion he didn't care to go into.

CHAPTER TWENTY TWO

A fog of tension loomed over the conference room at National Counterterrorism Center. The president of the United States sat in the seat in the center of the horseshoe-shaped table, under the seal of the NCTC and two rows of digital world clocks on each side of it. The heads of the CIA, FBI, DHS, and the State Department, as well as the president's national security advisor were all there. After they sat, they all took the president's cue and forced their respective smiles and thoughtful gestures for the flashes of the cameras before the meeting. This way, no black eyes or bloody noses would be apparent in the pictures that were to be made public.

"Ladies and gentlemen, I've decided to hold this briefing here at the NCTC instead of the situation room at the White House. The reason for this is that we have to emphasize unity. Unity of plan and unity of action. Recently, Nathan Anderson has made me aware of his frustration that, despite the NCTC's mandate for strategic planning and coordination of enforcement, not much besides bureaucratic data sharing goes on here." The president panned the table, making eye contact with each one of the chiefs. Bill Carpenter directed a glare at Anderson, then nodded for the president's benefit.

"That's why I'm going to direct the CIA and the FBI to each provide Nathan with a team of agents for coordination between planning and enforcement."

Ted Barnard, the director of the CIA, looked like he had just become constipated. Bill Carpenter's face was red as if he had just come in from four hours on the beach. Carpenter raised his hand.

"Bill?"

"Mr. President, your intentions are great, but aren't we curtailed by the legislation that established the NCTC? It doesn't have any enforcement capabilities."

"You're right, Bill, it doesn't. But NCTC has the primary responsibility for developing strategy for anti-terrorist law enforcement planning and operations, and that's not happening. We've got a four-year-old Congressional Report that says it should have the power to synchronize enforcement operations and compel specific action when required."

Barnard raised his hand. "Ted?"

"Mr. President, I agree with Bill. We can't have the NCTC out there doing its own enforcement. Plus, there's no budget for it." The other heads of agencies nodded theirs.

"I'm not suggesting that, Ted. That's up to the congress. But the authority for NCTC to coordinate efforts and to compel specific action is already in its enabling legislation. We have to stop competing and start cooperating. The two teams will remain a part of their respective agencies, but they'll work here with Nathan in order to coordinate our efforts. If the CIA or the FBI, respectively, receives a briefing that they decide to act on, they will follow normal channels. But if NCTC warns either one of you of an imminent threat, I expect your agency to act on it immediately, and with all available resources. Now this arrangement will be classified. None of this is for public disclosure."

The surprise part of the meeting behind them, Ted Barnard, gave a threat briefing, which showed no significant terrorist threats to the United States at the moment, followed by a briefing by Bill Carpenter on the progress of the investigation into the San Bernardino attacks.

"Bill, I want to assure you that your office has the full support of the White House in your investigation. Whatever you need. We must leave no stone unturned in determining why and how these terrorists carried this out."

"Thank you, Mr. President."

"Gentlemen, I think everybody here will agree -- we have the very best intelligence, counterterrorism, homeland security and law enforcement professionals in the world. Across our government, these dedicated professionals, including here at NCTC, are relentless, 24 hours a day, 365 days a year. At the operations center here, people from across our government work, literally shoulder-to-shoulder, pouring over the latest information, analyzing it, integrating it, connecting the dots. They're sharing information -- pushing it out across the federal government and, just as importantly, to our state and local partners. What I want to see here is one, strong, united team."

The president looked sternly at his disjunctive team of not-so team players. It was time to start working together so that there were no significant terrorist attacks during the remainder of his presidency.

Virginia felt the whoosh of hot air from the oven as she opened its door to check on the green bean casserole and baked potatoes covered in foil, and set them on top of the stove. It reminded her of opening the door to her apartment on a summer afternoon. The table had already been set with her finest stoneware (reserved only for guests) and the tapered candles were throwing off a warm yellow glow against the dancing shadows of the dining room wall. She had turned off the overhead lamp and the only supplemental light was provided by the table lamps in the adjoining living room. Nothing left to do but jump in the shower and make herself pretty. She would pop the steaks on the grill after Robert arrived.

Virginia showered, the cool water pulsating against her body, washing off the heat from the toil of the kitchen. As she toweled off, she went through her mental list of final preparations – appetizers, salads, main course and dessert. She examined her face in the mirror. Only thirty and she could see the signs of age creeping up on her. Doing her hair brought back the memory of the desert heat to her body and she felt like a second shower may be in order. But after she cooled down, she went into her makeup routine, applying a thin coat of foundation, smoothing it on lightly, then a bit of powder, blush for the cheekbones, and accentuated her eyelashes with mascara. A coat of lipstick on her pouty lips made the final touch. Keeping an eye on the time, Virginia hurried into the bedroom. She had told Robert that the dress code was casual, so she slipped into a casual summer dress, her favorite pumps, and regarded herself in the full-length mirror. This was as good as it was going to get. The doorbell rang.

Virginia opened her door to a man bearing flowers and a large, floppy-eared dog. She beamed, taking the flowers as

Robert greeted her and came in. The dog waited obediently on the landing.

"Come on in, Butthead."

The dog waltzed in, wagging his tail and lunging toward Virginia to get acquainted.

"Sit," Robert commanded, and the dog dutifully sat.

"He's cute!"

"He's ugly and scruffy, but at least he's clean. You should have seen him when he showed up at my door."

The dinner went off as perfectly as Virginia had planned, with the dog patiently and silently waiting for any leftovers.

"He's quite well behaved."

"I've been training him. Watch this. Come 'mere, Butthead."

The dog came to Robert and sat at his feet.

"Good boy. Now, show Virginia how you shake hands."

The dog put out his paw, then the other, and Robert awarded him with a small piece of meat, which he caught in mid-air. Then, Robert took the dog through his entire repertoire.

"He's so smart!"

Robert snorted. "Him? He's a dummy. But he'll do anything for food. This is the best one."

Robert balanced a piece of meat on top of the dog's brown nose, which twitched and fluttered, catching the scent.

"Awwww!"

Suddenly, the dog moved and the meat fell off his nose onto the floor. He gobbled it up immediately. Robert slapped him across his chops and the dog cried.

"Bad dog!"

"Julio!"

"He's not supposed to do that. He knows better than to defy me."

"Julio, it's normal for a dog to do that. He's just following his instincts."

For a moment, Robert's instincts were revealed.

Later that evening, the dog trick debacle had been long forgotten. Robert and Virginia relaxed on the couch. In the candlelight, she looked even sexier than he had originally thought, and the proximity of her body was making every nerve tingle as the pressure built up in his. Robert took the initiative, taking her soft, welcoming lips as she held on to his strong shoulders and he suppressed his bone crushing strength to hold her body with just the right amount of pressure that he had learned to use in these situations. Their kisses became more intense as he moved his hand to her breasts with no resistance. Her breathing intensified as he massaged them, but when he moved down lower, she held his wrist, signaling that she had reached her limit.

"I'm not quite ready for that yet. Can you wait just a few more days?"

Robert was already on the hunt and it had been a long time since he had a woman, but he stopped himself.

"Yeah, sure."

CHAPTER TWENTY THREE

Robert Garcia set out for Colorado on his KLR 650, leaning back on the Remington 700 in the guitar case. The camp was in rural Buena Vista, a town of about 2,600 people. With only three hotels in the village, Robert would be noticed, so he had picked up food and supplies in nearby Salida and set up his own base of operations within surveillance distance of the camp, which was a hodge-podge of small buildings, mobilehomes and trailers. An all-out raid on the camp would require a team of at least 7 men, but this would be a surgical operation using only one.

At about 5 p.m. that afternoon, a convoy of three Ford Explorers rumbled into the camp and came to a stop. Robert focused his field glasses on them and counted three security men (not including the driver) in the lead SUV, who exited their vehicle armed with AKMs and established a perimeter. Three more, similarly armed, hopped out of the third vehicle and two security men stepped out of the middle car. Bukhari and an associate Robert did not recognize from any of the reports exited the middle car and, surrounded by the security detail, were escorted to one of the mobilehomes. Four sentinels stayed outside to stand guard and the other four went inside with Bukhari and his charge. Robert could assume that security would be heavy throughout Bukhari's stay. With perseverance, patience, and a little luck, he planned to make Bukhari's respite brief, and to send him to paradise as quickly as possible.

Robert set up his 700 on its bipod. He calculated the distance at about 650 yards. That was doable for the Remington, but it would require a precise shot. At the moment, the wind factor was near zero, but that could change on a moment's notice. Robert planned to take his shot under cover of darkness, which made for a good getaway, but he had to take advantage of any opportunity that Bukhari could be exposed to his crosshairs, and that may mean broad daylight. He hoped for the former.

At dusk, two of Bukhari's security detail exited the mobilehome which probably signaled that Bukhari would be on the move. Bukhari and his friend evacuated the mobilehome next, followed by the last two armed guards. Robert followed Bukhari with his optics carefully, seeking the most accurate shot.

"Come on, a little to the right."

Suddenly, one of the guards stepped in-between Bukhari and the intended flight path of Robert's bullet.

"Shit!"

Robert patiently waited for another window, but Bukhari was whisked away in one of the SUVs before he had another opportunity to shoot. It looked to be a long night.

The convoy settled about 800 yards away, at another mobilehome. Robert looked through his sight and waited for the perfect opportunity to shoot. As they had established as their protocol, the guards in the lead vehicle exited, formed a perimeter, and the guards in the tail vehicle followed suit after the first two guards and then Bukhari and his buddy emerged from the middle vehicle. They were almost completely encircled by their security, but Robert only needed one fraction of a second to identify a shot, aim carefully and fire.

He got that opportunity just as Bukhari was about to enter the mobilehome. He was ascending several steps, which left his profile open. Robert aimed, fired, and blew his head off, toppling his body from the stairs. Two guards pounced on Bukhari's lifeless body while Robert aimed, fired, and hit Bukhari's associate in the head. They jumped to cover him as well, but he was already dead.

Robert heard the rat-a-tat of automatic fire from the AKMs and saw the muzzle flashes. They were firing at random, but it wouldn't take more than a minute for a small army of angry jihadists to spot and surround him. He had disturbed the beehive and the bees were furious. They poured out of the mobilehomes like cockroaches, adding more AKM fire to the mix as Robert quickly packed up his gear, saddled up and flew away with his lights off toward Mt. Princeton. There was only one road leading out of Buena Vista that went north or south. Robert stayed off-road and parallel to the 285 southbound. He would meet up with the 50 westbound at Poncha Springs.

The two SUVs with Bukhari's failed security team took off in pursuit and the one in which Bukhari and his associate had been riding sped them to the hospital in a futile attempt to save their lives. Robert looked in his rearview. He could not see the pursuing cars, but he knew that he had only about a ten-minute lead on them and that would most likely be lost because they were at highway speed and he was in the dirt. He still couldn't risk being exposed to local authorities or other pursuers that may have been alerted to his presence. He flipped on his headlight so he could pick up speed.

It was dark, but Robert's escape still put a cloud of dust behind him that was clearly visible from about a quarter mile away. He didn't know whether the trucks had gone north or south or split up, but there was no way of determining that because he had no air support. He stayed the course, pushing the motorbike to the limit even past the distance he could see in the headlight.

He saw some lights of cars on the neighboring highway, but nothing going at an abnormally high rate of speed, so he opted to rejoin the highway earlier and avoid being spotted by the side of the road. He could always go off-road again if they did see him. In the dirt, the KLR 650 would prove to be more agile and maneuverable than the bulky Explorers. Robert pumped his speed up to what probably was its limit at 100 mph, and checked the jittery rearview mirror for his pursuers. He spotted one pair of headlights far in the distance, which appeared to be going at an extremely high rate of speed. Robert passed several cars like they were standing still, and kept in the middle lane to use them to cover his position.

He could see the lone pursuit vehicle gaining distance on him. Their momentum was superior to the 650, which he was pushing past its limits, the RPMs off the charts. Robert could see them closing in on him, about a mile away, and gaining pace. He would wait until the very last possible moment before jumping off the highway, then lose them in the wilderness.

He spotted the Explorer closing in on him and could see muzzle fire from the side windows, signaling his time to exit the road. Robert leaped over the shoulder in a cloud of dust as he hit the dirt and watched in the side mirror as the Explorer jumped off road also. It had slowed some, but obviously had four-wheel drive, because it carried the desert floor with ease. Robert headed for high ground with the Ford on his tail, guns blazing.

He hit a series of berms, which would be a challenge for the Explorer but was child's play for the 650. Robert easily flew over them with alacrity, looking for more treacherous terrain to lose himself in. He looked in the mirror and saw the Explorer bouncing as it took the bumps, like a sailboat in rough water. As he approached a mountainous area, Robert dodged his way through large stones and bushes, which slowed him down a bit and the Ford a lot. He spotted a dark clump of evergreens and headed straight for them, watching the Ford bouncing and swerving behind him. Then, the Explorer hit one of the large stones and rolled over as Robert disappeared into the forest.

Robert headed deep into the wooded area for about 10 minutes, then parked, dismounted and quickly cleaned and buried the Remington under some soft dirt and stones, which took an extra 10 minutes off his schedule. Once it was done, he sped off, using his compass to connect back with the 50, knowing that the other team of pursuers and who knows who else may be looking for a lone man on a motorcycle. He had to dump it as soon as possible, but he still had mountain ranges to cross. His chances of hitching a ride were pretty slim at this hour, and the possibility of one of those rides being his pursuers was not one he was willing to take, so he planned to jam all the way to Grand Junction. There, he would dump the bike and pick up some alternate transportation. Paladine had, once more, dispensed death and escaped from it.

CHAPTER TWENTY FOUR

The alarms went off at NCTC and the watch team notified Director Anderson at his home. Colorado Springs Police had reported that Aqwa Bukhari and a key lieutenant of Al-Banwa had been killed by sniper fire. Anderson dressed and headed directly for the office in order to be briefed and prepare a statement for the press. He got on the line to Bill Carpenter, who ordered his task force out to Colorado. Paladine had taken out the number one terrorist on their watch list. It was time to take him seriously. This was a problem which had to be resolved by bringing him in – or otherwise dealing with him.

***

Joshua Maynard swung his bare feet off the bed and planted them on the floor. Another day of catching bad guys was about to begin. He stood up and shuffled into the kitchen and pushed the "on" button for the coffee machine, then headed for the bathroom, scratching his head and yawning. Joshua knew his priorities. When he was showered and ready for action, he filled up his mug with the second cup of the day and switched on his computer to check the news headlines on the Internet. Paladine had struck again. Aqwa Bukhari was one of the most watched men on the FBI's terrorist watch lists and a someone had just taken him out right under their noses. Was it for profit or for principle? Could there be any connection to the case he was working on? He jotted down the name of the investigator of the case in Colorado Springs. That would be his first call when he got to the office.

Joshua got into his Jeep Cherokee for the 30-minute drive from Chandler to Metro Phoenix. He had chosen to stay in the bedroom community so he could be closer to his two kids, even though it would have been more practical to get an apartment near work. It was his work that was the final breaking point of the marriage according to Sally. She used to complain that he was hardly ever home because of it. Now he never was.

Joshua passed the box of donuts on the table in the detectives' division and went straight to his office. It was Spartan – a working environment, with the only trace of humankind being the pictures of his kids on the desk, which were at least five years old. The décor of the office was non-existent. On the wall was a huge whiteboard on which he had made a collage of sorts – of evidence. In the center of the mural was a picture of Muhammad Abdul Kareem, the would-be metalhead suicide bomber. The only suspect was a fictitious character named Paladine. Surrounding the photograph of Kareem were case notes that Joshua had made. The other parts of the collage consisted of different cases. There were no connecting lines between any of the cases. Joshua picked up the black marker in the tray beneath the board and wrote a new name: Aqwad Bukhari. Then, under the name, he wrote: "suspected terrorist" and circled it. The word "suspected terrorist" had been written and so emphasized in each entry of the evidence board: Muhammad Abdul Kareem, Aqwad

Bukhari, Abdul Moussef (the McDonald's shooter), and Aaresh Shanahwaz, the terrorist who had been shot by a sniper at a mental hospital in California. All were suspected terrorists, and all had been executed by a person or persons unknown.

Maynard called Colorado Springs and talked to their detective in charge of the case, but there was nothing that he provided that Joshua hadn't already learned from the Internet. He called the local FBI office and spoke to the agent on duty. He explained the case he was working on and asked for access to the TSDB database, which he was given. When he asked about the Bukhari case, the agent gave him the names and contact information for two special agents from the Bureau who were working the case out of the National Counterterrorism Center. He thanked the agent and placed a call to Special Agent William Wokowski.

"Wokowski."

"Agent Wokowski, this is Detective Joshua Maynard, Phoenix P.D. I'm in charge of the Muhammad Adbul Kareem case here in Phoenix."

"The guy who tried to blow up the rock concert?"

"That's the one. I understand you're looking into the Bukhari case."

"Me and my partner, Jack Samuels."

"I've been looking at the similarities between all the suspected terrorists who've been murdered in the past three months."

"What have you found?"

"So far, that they're all suspected terrorists and they've all been murdered."

"In other words, not a lot."

"Well, my investigation is just beginning. I wonder if we may be able to compare notes?"

"Sure."

Wokowski vowed to cooperate any way he could with his investigation, and Maynard noted down his email address. He disconnected, then looked up at the whiteboard. Maynard stood up, picked up a red marker, moved his hand to the top of the board and wrote the name of his prey in block letters: "Paladine."

CHAPTER TWENTY FIVE

Robert never cared for social media, but in his work it was becoming more and more important. He had created a Facebook page under one of his Arabic aliases as well as a Twitter handle, and regularly surfed the pages of ISIS and other terrorist groups. Terrorism had gone high tech. No longer did it concentrate on developing personal relationships, or spend months finding and cultivating youngsters to join their deadly club. Now they could spread their propaganda online and the recruits would come to them already radicalized. Robert spent an hour or so every day, commenting, sharing and re-tweeting the jihadist rhetoric, mainly looking for more "inventory."

Farther west there was trouble hitting home with his employer. Bryce Williamson's foundation was run by a man named Rahbi Moghadam. Rahbi was originally from Syria, but had emigrated to the UK when he was very young. A successful software engineer in the Silicon Valley, Rabhi had quit his job and joined the foundation for personal reasons. His daughter, Rasha, had always wanted to help people. Although born in the UK, she strongly identified as Syrian and, at the age of 19, she learned of the Syrian civil war on social media and wanted more than anything to do something to become more involved in the humanitarian aid effort.

Unbeknownst to her parents, Rasha had met in person with an ISIS recruiter who had fed her everything she wanted to hear. He was young and handsome, and appealed to her romantic fantasies as well as her higher ideals. Rasha had decided that instead of goofing around for her summer vacation, she would spend a month in Syria, joining others in providing food and needed medical supplies to people suffering in her home country. She begged her parents to allow her a "study tour" in Turkey, and eventually they conceded. She was joined by two other girls on the flight to Istanbul and they made instant friends. They were all just as beautiful as they were gullible.

Rasha and her two friends were met at the airport by another handler and another girl from Eastern Europe. The handler helped them get across the border to Syria. The first thing he did was to collect their passports "so it would be easier for them to cross the border." Once across, he kept the passports and they were taken to an ISIS compound. Rasha found out right away that the type of humanitarian aid she was going to provide was as a sex slave in a jihadi marriage to six different ISIS fighters, who each raped her on a daily basis. Luckily, the compound was bombed and she and one of the others pretended to be Syrian refugees. Once across the border to Turkey, she found asylum at the US Embassy, who contacted her frantic parents.

Because there was no evidence tying him to the sex trafficking, and because of freedom of speech and religion, there was nothing the authorities could do about the local recruiter, who was still doing his thing. Rasha was an adult, after all, and had gone to Turkey on her own free will. After a year of intensive psychotherapy, Rasha killed herself. Rahbi, like Bryce, had selfish reasons for joining the foundation and had made himself indispensable to his boss. So, when he asked for a meeting in Bryce's office, Williamson naturally obliged.

Williamson received Rahbi and shook his hand warmly. He offered him a seat in front of the massive desk.

"Mr. Williamson, thank you for seeing me."

"Please, Rahbi, call me Bryce."

Rahbi smiled. "Bryce."

"Good, and my door is open to you at any time. You're an important guy to us."

"Thank you, sir. The reason why I asked for this meeting was a personal one."

"Oh?"

Bryce leaned forward and listened intently to Rahbi's story. He knew how helpless Rahbi felt, and he also could feel his need for revenge.

"So my reasons for joining the foundation weren't entirely all charitable. I know that your son was also a victim of terrorism, and I consider my daughter to be as well. That is why I have no choice but to ask you for a particular favor. If you refuse, I understand. I will resign if you like. But I want to get this jihadist scum who is responsible for my sweet Rasha's death."

Bryce looked puzzled. "How can I help you?"

"I'm very observant, Mr. Williamson – Bryce. I know that the man who killed your son was gunned down in Atascadero. I want the same thing for this asshole who killed my daughter. And I have money saved up, I can pay for it."

"Rahbi, you're assuming an awful lot. And what you're proposing is against the law."

"When the law fails to serve us, we must serve as the law."

Bryce could not express disagreement with that thought. But he also could not expose his relationship with Paladine, even to someone who was on the same side, as much as he wanted to help him.

"I'm sorry, Rahbi, but I don't think I can help you."

Rahbi hung his head. "That's alright, Mr. Williamson, I understand."

After Rahbi had left, Williamson slapped his palm against the office desk blotter calendar, crinkled it in his hand and squeezed it with rage, balled it up, and then threw it against the wall.

CHAPTER TWENTY SIX

What should have been a ten-hour ride had turned into a 20-hour ordeal. Robert had stayed over in Grand Junction, sold his KLR for cash to a junkyard dealer by turning over the signed, unregistered pink slip he had received from the guy he had bought it from, and bought a three-year-old KTM 990 from a private party. The KTM had a top speed of 129 miles per hour, could go zero to 100 in 3.2 seconds, and was well rated for off-road use. As Robert rode away on the 990 he thought that it would be a shame to have to dump it someday, but let that thought slide off his back. Possessions meant nothing to Robert.

When he got to Vegas, he went straight to the storage locker, parked the 990 and took his street bike home. As he was walking up the stairs to his apartment, he noticed a lump in front of his door where the welcome mat was supposed to be. It was that dog! The dog raised his pitiful face, hung out his tongue and wagged his tail as Robert opened the door.

"Well, you may as well come in." Robert directed his hand toward the open door in a sweeping motion and the dog shot up on all fours, and ran in, his tail going at the speed of an airplane propeller.

Robert filled up the bucket with water and set it on the floor. The dog ran to it immediately, lapping and lapping until his tank was full, and then dripping water from his chin all over the kitchen floor.

"Don't make me regret this."

The dog happily looked up at Robert, panting and wagging. Robert opened the fridge, which was virtually empty except for what was left of a twelve pack of Bud, so he closed it and rummaged the pantry for something to feed him. He found a box of crackers, poured them into a bowl, and set the bowl on the floor. The dog ran to the bowl and gobbled up the crackers, crunching crumbs all over the floor, then dutifully cleaning them up. The dog came over to thank Robert, panting in his face and licking him with his long, slimy tongue.

"Dude, you stink! Gonna have to give you a bath."

There was a knock at the door and the dog ran to it and barked loudly.

"Whoa, whoa, let's see who it is."

Robert went to the door and opened it a crack. It was the manager. The dog forced open the door and lunged out at him, sticking his growling muzzle in the manager's crotch. The manager froze in a ridiculous position.

"It's okay. Stand down."

"I, I thought you said you didn't have a dog."

"I don't."

The dog kept growling at a low purr.

"Can you tell him to back off?"

"Back off, Butthead!"

The dog immediately complied and the manager started rambling.

"If you're going to have a dog here, we need an additional security deposit."

Robert slammed the door in the manager's face. He patted the dog on the head. "Good job, Butthead!" The dog wagged his tail happily. He had found his keep.

Robert fired up his laptop and skimmed the stories about the Bukhari assassination. The second man he had shot was being groomed as Bukhari's second in command at Al-Benwa. A check in the world of the jihadi Darknet revealed that a bounty had been placed on Robert's head. Kill him and you get not only 72 virgins and paradise forever, but $100,000 to give to your survivors.

"How nice."

He turned his attention to the TSDB, focusing not at the top of the list, as this would be what they would expect. The terrorists weren't the only ones after Paladine after all – the feds would be too, and they may expect him to kill in numerical order. To Robert, they were all the same priority – another job, another 50k moved into the asset column. All in a day's work.

CHAPTER TWENTY SEVEN

Robert had friended hundreds of jihadists on Twitter and Facebook and had cultivated his farm regularly. He was a known figure under several aliases, but then undercover FBI agents probably were as well. The only difference between them and Robert was that he didn't pick the low-lying fruit. And, like Monopoly players who went to jail without passing go, Robert's targets skipped arrest and went straight to execution. Trolling for marks, Robert spouted jihadist rhetoric in Arabic, stating he lived in Southern California and wanted to kill as many infidels as he could for Daesh. It wasn't long before he received an inquiry for an encrypted chat by PGP.

"Hello, brother, may Allah be with you."

"And with you."

"I hear you are interested in joining the movement."

"Yes, I wish to fight here or in my homeland, which is Syria."

"There is plenty of work to be done here, brother. First we will need to discuss it. Do you have access to Skype?"

"Yes, I do."

"Good."

Muhanad Halabi was a Syrian-born US citizen with suspected ties to the Islamic State who lived in San Diego. According to the FBI, he was one of the most active ISIS recruiters west of the Mississippi. He had a not-so-insignificant place on the TSDB as a number four suspect.

Robert received an encrypted message with a Skype contact and time for a vetting video call. He assumed he would be a little older than the desired candidate, but his only purpose was to determine if this was Halabi or someone else who could be identified as a recruiter on the suspected terrorist database. There was no bounty for a dead undercover G-Man.

When the video call was initiated, Robert feigned problems with his video, but he saw the video feed from the recruiter clearly. It was a positive match for Halabi. Robert apologized for the technical difficulties, and Halabi advised him to send a PGP message once the video problem had been straightened out. Perhaps it was a problem with his Internet speed that could be corrected.

The intel on Halibi showed a last known address in Logan Heights. Hopefully, it was still accurate. He had been on the radar for quite some time now, but there had been nothing the feds could do about him. He wasn't dealing with underage girls or porn, just spreading the word of jihad to young, impressionable people, which, unfortunately, was not a crime.

Robert set out for San Diego on the 990. This would be a quick in and out job, and he planned on being back by daybreak, so he let the dog out to do his business and left him plenty of food and water at home. He took the I15 all the way to San Diego and exited the freeway in Logan Heights.

It was what Californians called a "rough neighborhood," and, in some respects, reminded Robert of El Barrio, except that there were more cracker box houses than apartment buildings. Robert located Halibi's house and cruised his neighborhood. He found a motel within walking distance and stashed the bike there in a parking space behind the building. Robert took a room for cash. The clerk didn't ask for ID. It was obvious this was a motel frequented by working girls because he asked Robert if he wanted the room overnight or for just a few hours. Robert got the room for overnight with no intention of staying after success of the mission. He slid the cash through the hole in the banker's window to the clerk and was given a key in return. There was the faint smell of urine outside as he unlocked the door to his room and he caught a whiff of mildew when he opened the door.

Robert set up his computer and accessed the Net through a WiFi server from a nearby beauty salon. He checked Halibi's Twitter and Facebook postings. It appeared that he had been actively posting every hour, so that indicated he must be at home.

There was no observation spot on the block where Robert could wait and stake out Halibi's place. He would just have to go in there and see what happened. He hit craigslist thinking he could pick up some kind of service uniform as a guise to get them to open the door and found a listing for a used postal service uniform and hat. That would do. He called the number in Escondido, got the address and went to pick it up. On the way back to San Diego, he dropped by a post office and picked up some express mail boxes.

Robert made his way back to the motel, stashed the bike, then took the short walk to Halibi's place wearing his USPS uniform. He knocked on the door.

A voice from inside called out, "Who is it?"

Robert smiled at the peep-hole and held up the Express Mail envelope.

"Post Office. Got an express mail delivery!"

A man opened the door, Robert silently shot him in the head and held his body as a shield, moving forward without a misstep. There were two others in the living room. He shot one and made a "shh" sign with his fingers to the other as he trained the pistol on him. He dropped the body and grabbed the other live one.

"Halibi!" He pushed him. A man came out into the corridor and Robert recognized him as Halibi. Suddenly, a large man came out of nowhere, pushed Halibi down and turned to Robert, reaching into his jacket. Before the big man could pull out his gun, Robert shot him in the head and chest. Halibi looked up at Robert and put his hands in front of his head, as if they would protect him from what was about to come.

"Please, please! Don't shoot me!"

"Have fun in Jahannam, asshole." Robert shot him two times in the head, then threw down his live shield. The man crouched on the floor and began to pray. Robert put the gun against the back of his head and fired.

He made a quick inspection of the house to make sure there was nobody else there, picked up Halibi's laptop and took his cell phone from his jacket pocket. This mission was over.

CHAPTER TWENTY EIGHT

Joshua Maynard received a lot more information from the FBI than he had expected, and the access to the TSDB database proved to be valuable to his research. With the exception of Aaresh Shanahwaz, every other murdered terrorist had shown up on their watch list, which meant that the shooter may have had access to it. That meant he could be in law enforcement, because that was the only type of person who had access. Maynard profiled the suspect from the information he had available. He was, most likely, ex-military Special Forces, because he was a sharpshooter. He could have equally been Mafia, but there were no other marks of organized crime on the case, nor were there any motives for any wise guy involvement. That meant he was probably either a gun for hire who had formerly been in the service, working for law enforcement with a military background, or currently in the service and working for one of Washington's first-string espionage teams.

Joshua booked a flight to Washington to meet with Wokowski and Samuels. If his suspect had a background in Special Forces, that would be the most logical place to start fishing for information.

Maynard made it to D.C. on time and was whisked away in a taxi to the National Counterterrorism Center, where he sped through security and was given a tour of the facility by Wokowski and Samuels. Maynard was impressed with the data and surveillance capabilities of the NCTC. If they only had half of the features in Phoenix they could probably rid the city of all crime in less than a year.

Wokowski and Samuels retired Joshua to a conference room, where they sat at a long oval table with sixteen chairs, and discussed his theories on Paladine.

"I think we're dealing with a highly trained individual, probably a mercenary who has a military background in Special Forces."

Wokowski nodded. "His expertise would certainly point us in that direction." He frowned. "If it's the same person who did all the killings."

"I think a lot of things point to it being the same person. The proximity of the killings to each other, the methods used, and the types of targets are all consistent with one another."

"So, how can we help?"

"I have access to the FBI's NCIC. That's a database I use all the time and I appreciate it. What we really could use in this case though is some hard analysis. We need to sort out the guys who have this type of expertise who have left the service and then break them down into the ones we can locate and the ones we can't. My gut tells me it's someone who's dropped off the grid."

Wokowski was eager to help. "You're in luck, Josh. We have the best analysts in the world working right here in this building. We can have them cull out your data right away."

"There is one other possibility."

"What's that?"

"It could be someone on the government's team."

"That would be illegal. Only the CIA can operate like that, and not domestically."

Joshua was not surprised by Wokowski's apparent naiveté. He was a respected FBI agent who was used to doing things by the book.

By the time Joshua was ready to leave he had been given the reports he requested, including photographs. He sorted out the ones who had seemingly disappeared from the face of the earth, which gave him his first eleven suspects. Eleven guys and any one of them (or none of them) could be Paladine. He skimmed the dossiers on each of them. One of the files was a certain Captain John Richards, aka Malik Abdul, aka Robert Garcia.

CHAPTER TWENTY NINE

The warm spring with its refreshing breezes had given way to the assaulting blasts of heat that marked the beginning of the Las Vegas summer. Robert had to set his clock early so he could take a morning run in Sunset Park. Once the sun peeked out above the mountains around 6 a.m., it wouldn't be long before the entire valley turned into a burning furnace. As he ran, with Butthead trotting at his side, panting and wagging, he contemplated his next move. He looked down at the dog briefly. He knew that this life he had made for himself in Sin City was only temporary. In Robert's life, everything was expendable. If the terrorists or the feds got too close, he would leave it all in an instant. There was nothing worth fighting for in Robert's life except for his own survival.

When Robert got in the door, he grabbed a bottle of water and drained it as he listened to the dog gulping water from the bucket faster than it could breathe.

"Slow down, dumbass!"

Robert took the bucket away from the dog, who stood in the place where it had been, choking and heaving.

"I sure as hell gave you the right name. You're no scholar." The dog looked up at Robert pitifully, water dripping from his chin like a waterfall in a pond.

Robert illuminated his laptop and continued his planning. The next most important targets (though not sequential) were clustered around the East Coast. It was time for Robert to go home. Most of the arrests so far that had been made by the FBI were of students who had expressed their desire to fight on behalf of ISIS in social media. They were then caught and arrested after the first move toward their plans, such as buying a gun. Nobody knew of Robert's gun purchases.

Robert selected his next target, a level one suspect by the name of Aasen Al-Zahawi. Zahawi was an ISIS loyalist who was suspected by the FBI to be Al-Baghdadi's right-hand man in the states. He lived in a one bedroom apartment in Queens, frequented by young people which would, most likely, be heavily guarded. This would be another silent operation. Robert finished his planning, committed it to memory, wiped out his external hard drive with a powerful magnet, then packed for his road trip. Just as he was about to leave the apartment, he realized that, as opposed to his habitude, he could not just walk out the door. He looked at the dog, which stood there like an idiot wagging his tail.

"You know, you're a royal pain in the ass, that's what you are."

Robert did a search for kennels and found one within walking distance.

Robert waved the dog out the door. "Come on, Butthead, let's go." The canine followed him faithfully out onto the deck, down the stairs and during the three-block walk to the kennels. Robert paid cash for a week's stay in advance, plus a little extra to overlook the blank spaces in his application form, and was finally off to New York.

The three-day ride was a little more comfortable on the KTM than his previous long haul to Colorado. The cycle was built to be equally comfortable on the street as well as off-road. Robert motored most of the day, from sunrise to midnight, and stayed in fleabag motels along the road at night. When he rolled into New York, he parked the bike in a parking garage. For the rest of his mission, he would rely on public transportation and his own two feet.

Robert was not the least bit nostalgic about being "home." New York City was just a place he had hung up his six-shooter for a while. He did not look up any old associates or "friends." For the few that existed, he was dead. But he did have an essential number memorized. He called it on a prepaid cell phone, arranged a meeting in half an hour and dumped the phone.

Tom Yankovic, if that was his real name, was a rusty old sailor and ex-Navy Seal who had found his retirement plan in the arms business. He was an "off-the-books" gun dealer who was on call for his customers, who were mostly assassins like him. Robert's meeting with Tom was set for a motel room in Queens. Robert would show up late because first order of business was checking the motel to make sure he wasn't being set up. It was far too short notice to orchestrate any kind of terrorist sting operation and an impossibly short amount of time for the feds, but Robert's paranoia had kept him alive this far and he wasn't going to let it desert him in his time of need. He walked the perimeter of the establishment listening with his parabolic microphone and looking with his infrared goggles. Everything appeared to be normal, so he double-checked room 16. Only one individual was in the room. He knocked on the door.

"Who is it?" Robert recognized the familiar, crackly voice of Tom Yankovic.

"It's me."

Tom opened the door with a bearded smile, and pulled Robert in as he shook his hand.

"Good to see you again, 007."

Robert nodded and Tom got right down to business.

"I've got just what you need. A selection of .22s to do the job and some nice automatics for contingency plans.

"Let's see your .22s."

Tom flipped open a large black briefcase which revealed five small handguns. He lifted one out and held it in his palm. "My suggestion: The Ruger SR22 with double and single action, 10-round magazine. Has its own special suppressor." Tom fitted a silencer on the Ruger and looked at Robert, who shook his head. The Ruger was a great gun, but he had used it in California and wanted to avoid similarities.

"No?" Tom put the Ruger and suppressor back into the case and withdrew a truly beautiful gun you might expect to be used by James Bond.

"The Walther P22. This is one bad ass piece of equipment. Only drawback to it is the side-mounted safety but I don't think that would interfere with your work."

He handed the gun to Robert, who held it in his hand, flipped up the safety with his thumb, pressed the magazine catch which dropped the magazine into his left hand, and slid open the chamber.

"Suppression?"

Tom lifted a silencer from the case. "Gemtech Seahunter. Best match for this little baby."

Robert fitted the suppressor onto the muzzle and looked through the iron sight. "I'll take it. Now, let's see your big boys."

Tom popped open another briefcase and smiled. He picked up one and fondled it. "For reliability and commonality, I strongly suggest the Gen 4 Glock 17. I'm sure you're familiar with this weapon."

Robert nodded and glanced at the rest of the pistols in the case. He picked up the Glock, popped out the magazine and opened the chamber.

"Would you like to see anything else?"

"No, this will be fine. I'll need suppression for this one too."

"This little beauty's been pre-threaded for a Titanium suppressor."

Tom handed Robert the silencer, and he screwed it onto the barrel. He nodded his agreement, which would be the only contract entered into between the two men.

"What do I owe you?"

"Four thousand."

It was more than three times the retail price, but people like Robert paid a premium for discretion.

"No prior ownership?"

"Negative. Both these specimens are brand new and personally tested by me."

Robert handed Tom the cash, tucked the pistols into his holsters, and took off.

CHAPTER THIRTY

Back at the office, Joshua Maynard pored over the files from the FBI and painstakingly researched each subject through every database he had available to him. Out of eleven, seven of them apparently had verifiable lives, jobs, and had been closely watched since leaving the service. These would be the easiest to check out, so Joshua went for the low-lying fruit if not for anything but to eliminate the less likely suspects.

He didn't want to approach any of them, in the slight chance that they may expose his investigation to Paladine, so he chartered around the fringes of their respective lives without leaving a trace of his investigation. Criminal background checks, job checks and credit checks were all done easily by computer and were below the radar. They would never know. The seven checked out. They all had jobs, bills and problems like any other normal person. They all had bank accounts with meager amounts in them. He couldn't check for cash under their mattresses, but Maynard assumed that what he was seeing was what he would get and moved on to the remaining four, which were more problematic.

These four suspects had many aliases, no bank accounts, no residence addresses, no jobs and no credit records that Joshua could locate. They all spoke Arabic and, at one time or another, had Arabic names. He wrote their last –known names on the whiteboard under "suspects." Jamal Abama, aka Ramul, Emanuel Lockman, Ali Salam and Robert Garcia.

***

Robert did his recon for the mission discretely. Early the next morning, he took a vantage point in an abandoned building across the street from the apartment and watched the comings and goings from what used to be an office in the old structure. The floor was dusty, the walls crumbling, and the windows had all been smashed. The walls were decorated with graffiti, and the remnants of its secondary tenants in the form of used condoms and garbage were strewn across the floor and it smelled like a gas station restroom.

Apparently, Al-Zahawi was holding court, because a lot of Arab teenagers would show up, get buzzed in, then remain there for hours. Robert scanned the one open window to the apartment with his field glasses. It appeared to have a large living room, kitchen, and one bedroom, which was behind the closed window to the right. Robert made adjustments to his attack plan and waited until nightfall. He shooed a mouse away from his knapsack and dipped into it to energize himself with high energy and protein foods he had bought at the grocery store. This was so he would not be seen coming and going.

From time to time, Robert saw two different young Arab men looking out the main window, and he surmised they must be sentinels. The first two high velocity bullets of the Walther had their name on them.

Once it was dark, Robert switched to his infrared goggles. He surveyed the apartment. There were seven heat signatures inside. The Walther had ten bullets in the magazine. If his shots were accurate, that would be sufficient. If not, he would have to use the Glock, which would be a little more messy. No time to change magazines in what Robert expected to be a pretty hot war zone.

At 2 a.m., one of the occupants left. Robert watched the man exit the main staircase of the building – it was not al-Zahawi. That left five inside. Two remained sitting, one at the door and the other at the window, two were prone on the couch and the two in the bedroom who had been actively engaged for the prior thirty minutes had settled down and were not moving anymore. If that was Zahawi, he had just been laid for the last time in his life.

Robert waited half an hour. The one by the door appeared to be slumped over, which meant he probably fell asleep, and the one by the window was seemingly still alert. He slipped out the back of the building, doubled back around, and went to the top of the stairs of Zahawi's apartment house. He rang a couple of random apartments, told the tired occupants that he had lost his keys, and was buzzed in.

There was one elevator to service all 11 floors. Robert used the stairs. Once on the fifth floor, he opened the access door slowly, peering down the corridor. As suspected, there was a sentinel perched by the elevator in a state of half-sleep. Robert walked up to him softly and took him out with one clean, silent shot to the head.

He took a ready position in front of the door to no. 216 and kicked it in with one smooth motion, shooting the sentinel to his left first and then the one near the window, who had just realized there had been a breach and did not even have time to reach for his weapon. He quickly shot the two occupants of the couch bed who were also just stirring and kicked open the bedroom door. What transpired then occurred in a fraction of a second, although Robert could see every detail as if it were in slow motion. Zahawi had heard the commotion, stepped out of bed, naked, and was holding a gun in front of him that he probably had kept under his pillow. Robert's weapon was pointed right at his skull. Before Zahawi could pull the trigger, Robert pumped two rounds in his head and two in the chest for good measure. The girl popped up from the bed, screaming. He shot her in the head and turned to leave.

Robert saw Zahawi's smartphone on the night stand and pocketed it.

"Allahu Akbar, asshole."

Robert left the bedroom, scanned the room, grabbed Zahawi's laptop off the desk in the bedroom, sheathed his Ruger and pulled out the Glock. He traversed the living room, then opened the front door to a barrage of gunfire in the corridor. Robert dropped to the ground, looking back and forth for the source of resistance. The gunfire was coming from the elevator. He shot two rounds toward the firing and waited for a pause which indicated the shooter was reloading. Upon hearing a few seconds pause, Robert slid into the hallway, propped up on his elbows, located his target and aimed. The shooter reloaded too soon and Robert took a stray shot of automatic fire in the shoulder. He completed his aim, fired, and blew three holes in the shooter's chest, propelling him against the wall in a bloody waterfall. Robert limped out, down the stairs and bleeding, into the night of the city that never sleeps.

CHAPTER THIRTY ONE

Robert put pressure on the wound. It was still bleeding, but not an arterial bleed, so he could still move around. He felt the back of his left shoulder but didn't discover an exit wound, which meant that the bullet must still be in there somewhere. It was too painful for him to ascertain if he had lost any range of movement.

Robert had to put as much distance between himself and Queens as possible, so at first he walked away as quickly as he could. He ducked into an alley, took a T-shirt out of his pack, and used it for a makeshift bandage. Then he headed for his old neighborhood in El Barrio. There was a dentist there known as Dr. D and he would have all that Robert needed.

When Robert reached Dr. D's door the night sky was just beginning to become light. Robert was numb to the pain but he was feeling weak and dizzy. The bleeding had slowed to a trickle. He rang Dr. D's buzzer. After a few moments, a tired voice answered.

"Who is it?"

"Dr. D, I need your help."

"I'll meet you in the office."

The door buzzed and Robert pushed it open and dragged himself to Dr. D's office in the main lobby. Dr. D lived in a flat upstairs. Robert had been there one time, not as a patient, but an observer. Dennis Carter, DDS, was a good dentist. He was also a gambler. Because of his habit, Dr. D, as he was known in the streets, would amass gambling debts from time to time. But he never had to worry about having his fingers or legs broken if he couldn't pay right away because Dr. D had protection. He would treat knife and gunshot wounds if they weren't too serious and, in exchange, the local riff-raff would cut him some slack. The doctor had all the necessary instruments to remove a bullet, stitch up a wound, and treat it with antibiotics to prevent infection, no questions asked.

Dr. D showed up moments later. He recognized the man leaning against his office right away, but didn't acknowledge it. He unlocked the office door and motioned him in.

Dr. D gave Robert some water to hydrate, then cleaned the wound and administered a local anesthetic. He removed the bullet and put it in a tray, then cauterized and stitched up the wound. He bandaged the shoulder, then put Robert's arm in a sling. He gave him a shot of antibiotics, and then offered him the bullet for a souvenir. Robert took it, not for memories, but to dispose of the evidence.

"How much do I owe you, Doc?"

Dr. D waved his hand. "Nothing."

"Don't be ridiculous." Robert reached into his pack and pulled out ten 100 dollar bills. They would last Dr. D a night on the tables, two if he was lucky.

"Thank you."

"Thank you, Doc. And remember, I was never here."

Dr. D smiled. "What are you talking about? I can't see anyone here."

***

Nathan Anderson called Samuels and Wokowski into his office.

"There was another hit last night on the Islamic State's number one man in the states."

"Al-Zahawi, we heard. Our guys in New York have been watching him."

"Well, I guess they weren't watching him closely enough. I want you two to go up there and see what you can find out."

"I thought we were here as the FBI's liaison to fight terrorism, not to locate this Paladine character."

"You are. I think it's all interconnected. Besides, he's making us look bad – all of us."

***

Joshua Maynard awoke, switched on the coffee machine, and went into the shower. He had an early plane to catch to San Francisco. It was a day trip, so, once he had showered, he suited up and prepared only his briefcase. Before leaving, he checked the news headlines on the Internet. Another suspected terrorist and his entire band had been hit last night in New York. The FBI and local police were investigating but social media had already solved the case – it was Paladine.

He caught Southwest Airlines' first flight to the San Francisco Airport. As he flew in, he looked out the window at San Francisco Bay and realized just how different it was from Phoenix – like another world. After deplaning, he bypassed baggage check and went straight to the shuttle for the car rental center. The air was crisp, cold and wet, not like the hot, dry atmosphere of Phoenix. Even in the summer, San Francisco was chilly. He shivered and pulled his jacket together as he boarded the shuttle train.

An hour later, Joshua presented himself in the reception area at Bryce Williamson's home office. The receptionist looked at him coolly.

"Sir, do you have an appointment?"

"No, I don't."

"Then I'm sorry, but I can't assure you that Mr. Williamson will see you. He's not well, you know."

Maynard whipped out his badge case and flipped it open to show her the instrument that usually cut through excuses like this. "I think he'll want to talk to me."

The receptionist picked up the phone and spoke into it. She set it down in its cradle and stood up.

"Please have a seat, sir."

After about five minutes of obligatory waiting, the receptionist stood.

"Mr. Williamson will see you now."

She led Joshua into Bryce's office, where he was seated at his desk, his nose hooked up to tubes from an oxygen tank. He appeared frail and like he should be in bed.

"Mr. Williamson, thank you for seeing me." He held out his hand and Bryce bent over his desk and took it, weakly.

"Detective Joshua Maynard, Phoenix Police Department."

Williamson's eyebrows raised. "Phoenix?"

"You're surprised, Mr. Williamson?"

Bryce coughed and sputtered. He indicated the chair with an outstretched hand. "Sit down, detective. Would you like some coffee?"

Joshua sat. "Yes, that would be great, thank you."

Bryce phoned the receptionist, and then set down the receiver. "What is it that I can do for the Phoenix Police Department?"

"Well, actually I wanted to talk to you about Aaresh Shanahwaz."

Bryce's jaw dropped. He coughed and hacked. "That piece of shit? May he rot in hell. But what does he have to do with Phoenix?"

"I'm working on a murder case there that I think could be related."

"Related? In what respect?"

"I think it may be the same shooter."

"You think the guy in your murder case is Paladine, don't you?"

"I do. And I also think that you hired him to take out Shanahwaz."

Bryce coughed again but didn't change his expression. He was better at bluffing than a champion poker player and his poker face was good enough to force anyone to lay down an otherwise good hand.

"That is a very serious accusation, detective."

"Do you deny it?"

"Unequivocally. Of course, I'd love to take the credit. Nobody hated that jihadist scum more than me. I'm sorry to have wasted your time."

The receptionist came in with a silver tray. On it was with one coffee cup, a sugar jar and a small creamer. She set it down on the desk in front of Maynard.

"You're not having any?"

"No. Drink up, detective. I hear it's pretty cold out there for people from out of town."

Joshua took a quick sip of his coffee and set the cup down, taking the hint that the conversation was over and that it was time for him to leave.

"You know, it seems to me that you're wasting a lot of resources looking for one man when he's doing your work better than you."

"I'm an investigator, not an executioner."

"Just the same, maybe you should leave him alone. Do you really care if another jihadist gets wiped off the face of the earth?"

Joshua didn't answer. He took another sip of his coffee. "Thank you, sir. If you change your mind and want to talk to me..." Joshua reached into his jacket for his business card holder.

"I won't."

Joshua set the card on the desk, took another sip and set the cup down. "Well, I left you my card just in case." He stood up.

"Jessica will show you out."

Joshua's meeting was brief but he was glad that he had come. He knew the old man was lying. All outward indications were that he was telling the truth, but he could feel it in his gut. He had come face to face with the employer of Paladine – at least for the Shanahwaz hit.

CHAPTER THIRTY TWO

Robert had to get out of New York more than he needed to sleep, so, as weak as he was, he took the 990 on the road for as long as he could, stopping at dusk for a meal and a motel bed in Gary, Indiana after a slight detour in Ohio to deposit the Walther and the Glock into deep storage in Lake Erie. Getting shot was always a possible occupational hazard, of course, but Robert normally never left a trail behind him to follow. This was a mess.

After scarfing down a steak and fries, Robert retired to his hotel room, took one of the sleeping pills Dr. D had given him, hit the pillow and was unconscious for the next eight hours. When he awoke, he made himself a cup of shitty tasting, watered-down instant coffee in the motel room's coffeemaker, used it to gulp down a pain pill, and opened his laptop. The news from New York was all over the headlines. The police and the FBI were investigating the murder of Aasen Al-Zahawi, six of his associates and a female companion. They had no suspects yet, but it was early in their investigation. He opened his TOR browser. There was an encrypted message from Bryce Williamson, asking for an urgent meeting. He scratched his forehead while he stared at the screen, then he powered off the computer without answering the message, packed up and left the room.

***

Wokowski and Samuels had hopped on the next plane to La Guardia, where they were met by their New York counterparts, Agents George Thompson and Alex Birnbauer, who took them directly to the crime scene, which was still being worked by the New York Police Department. The bodies had already been removed by the medical examiner's people, so Thompson and Birnbauer walked them through the scene, checking in first with the lead detective, David DeFasio, who was chomping on a hamburger.

"Detective DeFasio, these are agents Wokowski and Samuels from the bureau's office in D.C."

DeFasio, still chewing, offered his hand, which they tentatively took in tandem.

"Feel free to look around, gentlemen. My boys are just about done here."

Wokowski and Samuels took the lead in surveying the crime scene, while Thompson and Birnbauer tagged along. There were two victims in the corridor by the elevator marked by outlines in red tape, four in the living room of the apartment, and two in the bedroom – Zahawi and his female companion. They discussed the case with the medical examiner's technicians who were still on duty, and got an idea of the victims' fatal injuries. Samuels could see the gears rolling in Wokowski's head, so he hit him up for his opinion.

"So this guy takes out seven people just to get to Zahawi? How do you figure it went down?"

Wokowski strolled through the scene like Sherlock Holmes, piecing it together and re-enacting the crime, ignoring the forensic crew that was still dusting for fingerprints. He started in the corridor, examining the position of the two victims and the blood spatter evidence. Then he came to the door, looking to the right at the stairwell and the left at the elevator.

"I figure he must have come through the stairs."

"But isn't that inconsistent with him taking out the guard at point-blank range at the other end of the hallway?"

"Yes, but it's my hunch that he would have known there would be a guard there and didn't want the elevator bell to startle him. He probably waited for him to doze off and then tiptoed up to him and whacked him. This other guy in the hallway must have come later, because the shots he fired weren't as precise, probably automatic."

Wokowski examined the door to the apartment, which had obviously been kicked in. "Then he forced open the door." He made a "gun" with the fingers of his right hand and stepped in, swinging the make-believe gun left, then center, then right. "He took out the guard here, then the guy at the window, and the two on the couch in less than two seconds, and then he breached the bedroom."

Wokowski stepped into the bedroom, shot left and then right.

"Zahawi barely had enough time to get out of bed when the shooter shot him, then the girlfriend, and then he was out."

"What about the second guy in the corridor?"

"From the position of the body, it looks like he was hit while he was charging, not like the guard, who was probably asleep. I figure he was last – maybe he came on the scene after it had already gone down and tried to stop our guy, who shot him and probably escaped down the stairs the same way he came up."

Wokowski and Samuels moved toward the stairs, followed by the other G-Men.

"Wait!" Wokowski held out his hand to stop Samuels in his tracks.

"See that?" he said, pointing at the staircase landing.

"Yeah." They all nodded.

There were some reddish-black drops, which had soaked into the porous surface of the staircase.

"That's blood. Our guy must have been hit."

Wokowski called Detective DeFasio and what was left of his forensic team over to take samples, and then followed the blood trail out into the street, where it disappeared.

"If our dude has a DNA record anywhere, he's toast."

CHAPTER THIRTY THREE

The return trip had taken longer because Robert had to stop more often for rest. He made it home late, and darkness was the perfect cover to store the 990 and take his street bike home without anyone noticing. He checked once more on the Internet and found another message from Bryce: "Need to see you." Robert replied: "Negative, waiting for things to settle down." Robert drank some water and had some stale crackers, which is the only thing that he could find in his empty cupboard, besides the dog food he had purchased for Butthead. He hit the bed without showering, exhausted from the entire ordeal. His shoulder was killing him, so he popped some pain pills that Dr. D had given him.

***

Jason Maynard's morning at the office began by reviewing the crime reports and evidence of the New York shooting he had received by email from Agent Wokowski. Satisfied in his gut that it was connected to the other hits, he put it on the whiteboard. He sat in his chair and studied the board, as if he were playing chess and contemplating his next move. He was.

Maynard hit the Net and made further search inquiries into the *John Williamson Foundation to Fight Terrorism*. The Foundation's website boasted prominent corporate sponsors, like Wells Fargo Bank, Walmart, and Chevron. Freshly posted articles outlined the gun control bill which was being sponsored by Senator Rubinstein and another proposed bill in its infancy for stricter immigration screening, promoted by a prominent congressman. He dug deeper, delving into the bowels of the Darknet and found the companion underground site of the foundation, which advocated the idea of changing the laws to allow the federal government more leeway to summarily remove suspected terrorists, by assassination if necessary.

Even though the Dark web articles were more radical, none of them promoted criminal behavior. They did, however, glorify the mysterious Paladine and applauded the apparent vigilante for his valiant efforts. Maynard thought Paladine was just the opposite of a hero – a professional killer – which supported his hypothesis that it was Williamson, the founder and main benefactor of the foundation, who was pulling his strings. Using the resources offered him by the federal government, he snooped into Williamson's email. There were no suspicious communications, coded or otherwise, only business correspondence and a small amount at that. Williamson did not appear to be much of a computer person. Maynard had noticed when he was in Williamson's office that there wasn't even one on his desk.

***

Wokowski and Samuels briefed Nathan Anderson at NCTC's offices on their findings in New York. Anderson was excited

154

about the fact that blood had been found in the stairwell but he kept that to himself. Wokowski was worked up enough to follow the leads on the case without Anderson appearing to have tunnel vision to catch Paladine.

"Great work. Maybe you should compare notes with that Detective out of Phoenix, what's his name?"

"Maynard."

"Yeah, Maynard."

"We're already on it; paying a visit to Maynard tomorrow."

"Good. Let's also be proactive and make sure that we're keeping an eye on all the guys who are class 1, 2 or 3 on our list."

"Already done."

Anderson liked Wokowski. He had finally found comfort in his new assignment. Now for the real prize – to catch Paladine.

***

Unaware of but suspicious of law enforcement activity, Robert rose early and took a walk to buy supplies and pick up the dog. When he arrived at the kennel, the dog was more excited to see Robert than the bag of groceries he was carrying. He cried and jumped around and carried on like he hadn't seen Robert in years. When they got to the front door of the apartment, Robert could hear the phone ringing inside. He opened the door, set down the bag and the dog ran to it and stuck his head in it, sniffing. Robert picked up the phone and said hello.

"Hey, where have you been?"

155

"Hi, Virginia. I've been away on work the past few days."

"No kidding. I've been worried about you. Why don't you get a cell phone like everyone else in the 21st century?"

"So I can be a slave to those things? No thanks. I'd rather have a ring around my nose."

"Well, at least I would have been able to text you. How are you?"

Her voice didn't sound nervous, only concerned, which didn't bother Robert.

"I'm actually a little under the weather."

"What's wrong?"

"Nothing, nothing. Just a little shoulder pain. It'll go away."

Robert couldn't possibly advance their relationship past friendship at this point. Once he took off his shirt, there would be no explanation other than the obvious for the gunshot wound. But it was pleasant to talk to her.

"When can I see you?" she asked, inquisitively.

"How about dinner tomorrow night?"

"Sounds good."

"Pick you up at eight?"

"Great, and feel better."

"Thanks."

Robert disconnected. He looked over at the dog, who was panting with his dumb tongue out and wagging his tail. With relationships came responsibility. And danger.

CHAPTER THIRTY FOUR

Joshua Maynard received Agents Wokowski and Samuels among the inquisitive stares of his co-workers. They were obviously feds and none that they recognized. The three sequestered themselves in Maynard's transparent office with its glass wall, which enabled his colleagues to sneak glimpses at them as if they were watching fish in an aquarium.

Maynard walked Wokowski and Samuels through the notes on his whiteboard and discussed his theories that the same shooter was involved in all the shootings and that at least one of them – and probably all – were financed by Bryce Williamson, who had a hard-on for terrorists because his son had been a victim of an attack. The only catch was he had been unable to uncover any evidence connecting the two, not to mention the identity of the shooter himself. He spread out the files of his four suspects on his desk.

"These guys are all ghosts." Maynard threw up his hands. "And we still have to check out the others who are possibly in law enforcement."

"We've cleared them," Samuels said. "We'll give you the details."

Wokowski browsed Maynard's files. He had studied them before he turned them over to Maynard but took a second look just the same. "Well, it would be easier if we had a DNA match on the blood in the stairwell."

"No record?"

"Nothing."

Disappointed, Maynard paused and put his knuckle to his cheekbone, as if that helped him think. "Then we've got to run down each one of them. This one, Abdul Jabama, was a witness in a recent court-martial out in California. I've ordered the transcript."

"Good," said Wokowski. "Maybe it'll give you some leads. For now, we're pretty much at a standstill."

"And while I'm waiting for the transcript, I'll just go down the line – Lockman, Salim and Garcia."

Maynard filled them in on his discussions with Bryce Williamson and his Internet research. After about an hour's discussion, they declined his offer for lunch and bid him farewell. When Maynard escorted them out of his office, all eyes seemed to look up curiously, then back down. Maynard noticed and smiled to himself.

Later, while Maynard was munching on take-out pizza that the collective had ordered, a large box was delivered to him by FedEx. He opened the box and pulled out the transcript from the Ryan Bennington court-martial. He set the haystack on his desk and began leafing through it for the needle.

**

Robert tended to avoid the Strip, but it was fun to look at from afar, so he booked a table for dinner at the Alize at the top of the Palms Hotel. The Alize was a fancy French restaurant which had a 360 degree view of the lights of Las Vegas Boulevard. For the occasion he even wore his one and only sports jacket, which held a dual purpose, just in case his wound bled through his shirt.

The waiter led them through the modern, but richly adorned tables to a place by the window. Robert pulled out the chair for Virginia, who smiled up at Robert as she adjusted her stunning black cocktail dress to be seated. They dined on the seven course tasting menu. Robert had the impression the twinkling lights of the Strip were reflected in Virginia's eyes. The sommelier asked if they would like some wine. Robert knew nothing about wine. He was a beer man, so he let the man suggest a selection of wine to go with each small course.

Halfway through the meal, they were completely full.

"Sorry to say this, but I don't understand the point of an elegant restaurant stuffing you like a pig."

Virginia giggled. "Maybe they're plumping us up. There's a witch in the kitchen and she's going to shove us into the oven."

Robert smiled. "Not on my watch."

They caught up on things, with Virginia sharing more of her life and Robert reciting the canned answers from his fictitious background in response to Virginia's questions.

"Have you heard about this Paladine terrorist killer?"

Robert almost spit a mouthful of wine. He coughed and put his napkin to his lips. "No."

"Of course not. No cell phone, you probably don't have a computer, either, do you?"

Robert shook his head. The last thing he needed to do was create an email trail.

"He's like this super hero, you know? He tracks down terrorists and kills them before they can hurt anybody."

Robert was amused with the positive spin that had been placed on his path of mayhem and destruction.

"And they're trying to catch him. I think that's terrible! He's actually doing a better job than they are!"

That comment brought Robert back to the stark, cold reality of what was his existence. Up until that moment he had enjoyed being there in her company. Now he realized that he had been kidding himself he could have some kind of a relationship, and this moment was fleeting, slipping away, like everything else in his life.

CHAPTER THIRTY FIVE

Maynard studied the court-martial transcript, which had detailed testimony from Jamal Abama, one of the suspects, as well as an unknown "John Doe." Maynard called the attorney for the court-martial defendant, Brent Marks, but he refused to reveal the identity of the mysterious John Doe.

Jamal Abama had been a sergeant in the US Army before serving for Special Forces under the command of Colonel Jeffrey Steelman. In the trial, he claimed to be part of a death squad, commanded by Steelman to kill whole groups of people which the CIA's intelligence had identified as insurgents or insurgent sympathizers in an attempt to crush opposition to Shiite factions. All of his assignments for Special Forces were assassination jobs.

The testimony of the witness known as "John Doe 1," who had been allowed to testify in court under an alias for his protection was even more chilling. John Doe told the unbelievable story of the things he had done under Steelman's command. Doe and the men on his death squad spoke only Arabic and dressed in native clothing. Under Steelman's direction, they had wiped out whole camps of insurgent sympathizers, masquerading as Arab militants or jihadists.

They even beheaded their victims at times. Maynard naturally pondered the question whether Doe himself was actually one of the seven suspects. Both he and Abama fit the profile, and both had served on death squads under Steelman.

Maynard called Major Brinkman, the prosecutor on the case, who gave the not-so-useful description of John Doe 1 as a dark-skinned, bearded man of average height. He had no clue of the man's nationality or background, other than the fact that he could speak fluent Arabic. This did not help Joshua nail down which suspect in his file could be Doe, or if he was even in that lineup.

Maynard checked with Wokowski on the current whereabouts of Abama. The last record they had of him living anywhere was before he had enlisted in the Army, and that was in Sterling Heights, Michigan, so Maynard booked a flight to Detroit to check it out.

***

Williamson kept insisting on contact with Robert, but Robert resisted. Finally, Williamson sent an ultimatum:

"Advance deposit was based on fulfillment of obligations. Must be returned if you fail to perform."

Robert thought carefully, then typed: "I will perform."

He opened Zahawi's laptop. The browser history had been erased, but he wasn't worried about that. Zahawi had made the mistake of keeping data on his hard drive, something Robert never did. He spent several hours going over it, recovering, with a few tech tricks he had learned, even information from the disk that had been erased.

From reading the drive, Robert understood that the Islamic State was planning a large organized attack, the likes of which had never been known since September 11th. What was more important than that to Robert was that it also contained the identity of ISIS operatives all over the United States. Suddenly, the dog made a whining noise and Robert looked down at him. He was wagging his dumb tail and sporting a pitiful begging face.

"What?"

He looked down at the dog and went back to reading. The dog slavered and smacked, and whined again.

"What do you want?"

Robert looked back at the computer. He felt a cold, slimy nose nudge him under the elbow.

"Hey!" Robert looked at the dog, then at the computer screen. The clock in the corner read 10:43 p.m. Then he realized what it was.

"You're hungry! I'm sorry, boy."

He went to the cupboard and took out the bag of dog chow. The dog jumped and wagged his tail so hard Robert thought it would fly away. He poured the food into the bowl and the dog scarfed it down. Robert went back to the computer.

Unlike Halibi's computer, Zahawi's was full of useful information, almost too much for Robert to memorize. Still, he couldn't afford to have it lying around. There were not many details of the organized attack that was being planned, but enough to reveal to Robert that major financial centers and energy providers on the eastern seaboard were possible targets. As with the September 11th attacks, they were aiming at crippling Wall Street, the symbol of western decadence and aggression.

Robert had no doubt that the higher-ups at the Islamic State were probably not religious and didn't give a crap about Allah or Islam or the poor people they exploited. They had institutionalized terrorism as a political tool and were using it for their own profiteering, much like the politicians in the United States who had started the most vicious cycle of holy wars since the Crusades with their invasion and abandonment of Iraq and the assassination of Khadafi. He spent the rest of the day reviewing the information on the hard drive, then wiped it clean, smashed it, and threw it in a dumpster at a grocery store near the Strip.

When he got back home, he made a last-minute check on his own computer, and found another encrypted message from Bryce.

"Must see you."

Robert shook his head and wrote: "Impossible. Must wait."

Talk below the line on the Darknet and above the line on the traditional Internet and conventional media was all about Paladine. ISIS, Hamas, Nusra and Al-Qaeda had all sent messages and videos telling their "soldiers" to seek him out and eliminate him, which made Robert chuckle. They vowed to bring a reign of retribution upon the United States and Europe, the likes of which they had never seen before. That just made him angry.

CHAPTER THIRTY SIX

Maynard discovered soon enough that Sterling Heights, although it appeared to be a typical suburban Midwest town, had an Arab section that was probably the largest in Michigan besides Dearborn Heights. Using the last known address of Abama that had been registered with the court-martial, he knocked on the door of the apartment manager. A white woman, about 60ish, opened the door a crack, looked at him over the chain and spoke to him in an unusual drawl.

"Hello, can I help you?"

"Yes, ma'am, I hope you can. I'm Detective Maynard from the Phoenix Police Department and I'm looking for a man who used to live here by the name of Jamal Abama. Maynard flashed his badge and she unchained the door and opened it completely.

"Phoenix, huh? You say the fella's name was Abama? Don't have anyone o' that name, present or past."

Maynard took a picture from his jacket and held it up for her to see. "Are you sure you don't know him?"

The lady lit up. "Well, that there's Ramul. Yeah, he used to live here 'til 'bout six months ago, then he moved."

"Have any idea where? Did he leave a forwarding address?"

"No, but I got's a reference from him when he moved in."

"Can I see it, please?"

"Just a minute."

The lady left and came back a few minutes later with a 3x5 card with some information penciled on it. "Here it is, he gave Miss Abigail Walker as a reference."

"Is her address there?"

"Yup. 340 South Bender Street, Sterling Heights. Her phone number's here too. I called it to check him out when he rented cuz I don't trust just anybody off the street to rent an apartment. I rent to a freeloader and I get fired."

"Yes, ma'am. May I have the card, please?"

"Sure, I don't need it no more." She thrust out her hand and Maynard took the card.

"Thank you, ma'am."

Abigail Walker was at work when Joshua called her, so he arranged to meet her during her lunch break at a little cafeteria in her office building. She was small and soft-spoken, not at all the type you would expect to be associated with a deadly assassin. Walker had a tray of food from the cafeteria, but wasn't touching it. Maynard sipped on a cup of coffee as he spoke to her.

"Why is the Phoenix police looking for Ramul?"

"We just need to ask him a few questions about a case I'm working on – it's just routine. Do you know how I can contact him?"

"Well, I do, but I'm not sure he'd want me giving out his number. Besides, I don't think Ramul's ever been to Phoenix."

"Was he out of town on the fourth of last month?"

"He hasn't been out of town since he went to that trial in California. What day was the fourth?"

"Friday."

"Ramul was with me that Friday. In fact, Friday is our usual night out and he never misses it. Not since he's been sober."

"He have a drug problem?"

"Had, he's a recovering addict. He knows I won't see him unless he's sober."

"So, I assume he's staying with you now?"

She averted her eyes and looked down, then up. "Why would you say that? I didn't tell you where he was."

"If I could just talk to him, Miss Walker. He's in no trouble so long as your alibi for him holds up."

She looked offended. "My alibi! I told you he was with me!"

"Yes, ma'am, you did. And that gives me no reason to treat him as a suspect. But I still would like to talk to him."

"What's this all about?"

"That's police business, Miss Walker. Ramul may know something that may be important to the case."

"I'll talk to him."

Maynard took a hotel in Sterling Heights. Part of police work was patience – patience and persistence.

***

Nathan Anderson leaned back in his leather executive chair and looked down at the high-tech great room of the NCTC. It had been weeks since the president had assigned him a two-man team of FBI agents and a two-man team of CIA men. He hardly ever saw the CIA agents and his relationship with them was one of giving information rather than sharing. But the FBI team was a little easier to work with – maybe because of the embarrassment their boss had suffered over the San Bernardino debacle. The terrorists in that case were on both watch lists – TIDE and TSDB – but were cleared as potential threats by the bureau – twice. Carpenter was giving Anderson a lot of slack on this assignment. This way, if there was any screw-up, it would be on his head, not Carpenter's. Nathan thought it a brilliant political move, although he had his own selfish reasons for more enforcement control. Having only two agents was a joke, but it gave him two more field workers than he had before.

Wokowski and Samuels showed up on time for the briefing and with a detailed report of their findings in New York. They, too, had picked up an itch to catch Paladine and had hit their databases like mad to try and pick up his scent. It was a major setback that there was no DNA record of the suspect's blood, but that would have been too easy.

"What about that detective from Phoenix?"

Wokowski looked up from his report. "Who, Maynard? What about him?"

"Well, it seemed to me he had a real interest in our suspect and, well, he's kind of like a bloodhound."

Wokowski frowned as Anderson continued. "No offense to our nation's best, but it seemed to me that this guy's the type that never gives up. Are you comparing notes with him?"

Samuels piped up. "We are, sir. We even went out to Phoenix to meet with him."

"Well, see what he's been up to. He's looking for one suspect, but for us it's about the big picture – wiping terrorism from the face of the planet."

***

Maynard's endurance paid off. He received a phone call, not from Abigail Walker, as expected, but from Jamal Abama himself.

"This is Jamal Abama. You wanted to talk to me?"

"Yes, could we meet?"

"I think it's fine on the phone."

"Suit yourself. Let's get one thing out of the way first, okay? Where were you Friday the fourth of last month?"

"I was here, with Abigail. She told you that."

"Relax, I had to ask. I read the transcripts of the court-martial trial and I know what kind of work you did for Special Forces."

"Yeah, so what?"

"So what is that the suspect I'm looking for has the same type of special skills and training as you."

"I ain't givin' anybody up."

"Then you do know someone who fits the profile."

There was silence on the phone.

"You know someone?"

"If I did, I would never give up a brother."

"Even if it meant putting yourself in the clear?"

"Even if. And, besides, I thought you said I *was* in the clear."

"An alibi is only as good as its details."

"I ain't got nothin' more to say."

Maynard wasn't discouraged by Abama's lack of cooperation. His acknowledgement and the fact that the transcript also contained testimony from another Special Forces commando kept him going.

"You know, I read the entire trial transcript."

"So?"

"I know that both you and the witness they called 'John Doe 1' served under Colonel Jeffrey Steelman. And I know what you both did."

"So talk to Steelman."

Maynard ignored the comment. He had tried to talk to Steelman, but Steelman had pawned him off on his attorney.

"I'm talking to you. Who is this John Doe 1?"

Another silent pause. "Who is John Doe 1?"

"I told you, I got nothin' to say."

CHAPTER THIRTY SEVEN

New York was the next whistle stop on Joshua Maynard's itinerary. Wokowski and Samuels had been very helpful in briefing him on their findings, but there was nothing better than talking to the chief investigator in a case. The 104th Precinct in Queens was a free-standing brick building that made Joshua imagine what it must have been like working as a police officer in the 1920s.

Joshua was received by Lieutenant DeFasio. DeFasio had a belly from driving the desk too long but didn't seem to be overly concerned about his appearance. He waddled Joshua into a cubicle sized, fishbowl office and shut the door. DeFasio took a seat and held out his hand toward one of two metal chairs in front of his grey steel desk and Maynard took a seat.

"So what brings you all the way out here from Phoenix?"

"Like I told you on the phone, I'm working a case back home that I think may be related to the Zahawi case."

"Yeah, you said you've also been talking to those two feds who ran over my crime scene. I didn't much care for their attitude." DeFasio picked at his fingernails.

"I'm not here to offend you or to step on any toes. I just wanted to talk to you and see what you had that may have a bearing on my case."

DeFasio shrugged his shoulders. "You're welcome to look at my case files."

Joshua reached into his briefcase and put his own suspects file on the desk. He took out the seven photos and dealt them like a poker hand one at a time to DeFasio as he spoke.

"These are the suspects that fit the profile. I just talked to this guy – Jamal Abama – in Detroit. He's got an alibi for my case from his girlfriend."

DeFasio snorted. "Probly has an alibi for every one of 'em."

"That's what I thought, too, but he called me back and was pretty straightforward. Except when I started asking him about John Doe 1."

"Who's John Doe 1?"

Maynard outlined the high points of his investigation for DeFasio, including the court testimony of Abama and John Doe 1."

"Sounds like this John Doe guy is afraid of being hunted by the feds."

"Yeah. There's a lot of those guys out there. All they've learned how to do is to kill people and that's the only thing they're good at. They hang around conflicts, serve as mercenaries. But the things they do – it takes a toll on an average person – turns them into something else."

DeFasio smiled. "Sounds like you're buying into this super hero shit. What are they calling him? Paladine?"

Joshua looked DeFasio in the eye. "I think he's nothing more than a glorified hit man. And I intend to track him down and bring him to justice."

DeFasio made a face. "I dunno. The way I look at it is, if this guy really is targeting terrorists, and this ain't some random collection of remarkably similar cases, why not let him do his thing? Cleaning the streets of this terrorist scum is something we could never do, what with our court system and laws and such. They got too many rights."

Maynard disagreed with DeFasio, but it was irrelevant. He was just saying his piece. He could see beyond DeFasio's attitude that he was a good police detective who would not turn his back on the case just because he felt that wiping terrorists out was a good thing.

DeFasio brought Maynard up to speed on his investigation, but there was one detail that piqued his interest.

"So you didn't expect to find any records of treatment of the suspect's gunshot wounds, of course, because it would have to be reported. But he'd have to have been treated somehow."

DeFasio grinned at Maynard. "How do they do it on your side of the tracks?"

"Usually there's a veterinarian or someone who will take out a bullet and sew up a wound."

"Same here, but it's a little different. The underworld has their own little network of people with skill sets that match their needs, except here it works like it always has since the 30s. The wise guys run protection or gambling or what have you. Or they collect bad debts. Anyway, if it's a pro like a doctor or dentist who brushes up against these bad guys and

173

gets in some trouble, they'll cut him a break instead of breaking his legs if he agrees to sew up their guys with no questions asked."

Maynard put his thumb to his chin. "So if we were to lean on some of these characters, maybe we could get some leads."

DeFasio shook his head. "These guys are in bed with the mob. You hang a jail rap over them guys and they'll pick it over a coroner's refrigerator with a tag on their toe every time. Plus, there's a lot of 'em out there."

"You just bring in the ones who've had brushes with the law. The alcoholics, the addicts, the gamblers..."

DeFasio laughed. "You think that narrows it down? I've yet to meet a doctor who isn't an alcoholic. But, still I think it's a great idea. I'll have my guys cull out a list and I'll lean on each one of 'em personally."

Maynard thanked DeFasio, who promised he would keep in touch. He had a couple more stops to make before heading back to Phoenix.

***

Robert took off the old bandage and examined his wound. It was turning purple, but other than that, it didn't look so bad. No puss or discharge. He winced as he doused it with alcohol and put on a fresh bandage that he had picked up at a local drugstore. He popped one of the antibiotic pills that Dr. D had given him and went back to work. Bryce Williamson had answered and made it very clear that it was in Robert's interests that they meet in person. The question was how and where.

CHAPTER THIRTY EIGHT

Maynard planned to fly to California to meet with the court-martial prosecutor before heading back to Phoenix, but first he checked in with Agent Wokowski. He brought him up to speed on finding and meeting with Jamal Abama, but what he really wanted to know was whether they had turned anything up on the other two suspects – Emmanuel Lockman and Ali Salim.

"Negative. Lockman was pulling security duty with a defense contractor in Iraq but we lost track of him about a year ago. Same with Salim. We'll just have to keep looking."

Maynard was disappointed, but determined to run down all the leads, starting with John Doe 1.

***

Major Theodore Brinkman was the Judge Advocate General in charge of the prosecution of Captain Ryan Bennington, the case in which John Doe 1 had testified. Brinkman was happy to receive Joshua Maynard in his small office on the Fort

Hunter Liggit Army Base in northern California, but there wasn't much he was willing to say. Maynard sat across from Brinkman at his desk. He glanced at the stark walls, which contained only framed diplomas from law school, his license to practice law, and his military wall plaque.

"I sympathize with you, detective, I just can't reveal to you the identity of John Doe 1."

"Well, it won't hurt to go over the suspects with you, will it?"

As Brinkman shrugged, Maynard took out the photographs of the seven and flipped them in front of Brinkman, one by one.

Like a technician with a polygraph machine, Maynard examined the major's reaction to each of the headshots. He purposely set Jamal Abama's photo in front of him as the "control shot" and watched him react.

"You recognize him, of course."

Brinkman nodded. "Jamal Abama."

He remembered Brinkman's reaction to the photo in order to measure it against his expression when he saw the other pictures. Maynard threw out number two, then three, four, five, and six – which brought the raised eyebrows that Maynard was looking for. He tapped on the face.

"And this is John Doe."

Brinkman said nothing. He averted his eyes. "I told you I couldn't reveal his identity."

"You just did."

***

In his excitement, Joshua Maynard called Agent Wokowski on the ride to the airport.

"I found John Doe 1. It's suspect number seven – Robert Garcia."

"That's great! I'll run his photograph through the facial recognition software and try to pick him up on public records. Can't promise anything, but I will let you know what I come up with."

For the first time in weeks, Maynard felt satisfaction. It was worth all the bitching his boss had been doing about him spending too much time on the case. It was worth all the complaining his ex-wife had been giving him about not seeing the kids as often. Once he solved this case they would realize why he had to make those sacrifices.

CHAPTER THIRTY NINE

Robert should have been resting so he could heal, but Bryce's appeal to him was pretty strong. He dropped the dog off at the kennel and hit the road for San Francisco. When he arrived, he taped a prepaid cell phone to a dumpster on 30th Street, and then headed for the nearest coffee shop with free WiFi.

It wasn't hard to find one – there was a Starbucks at every corner – so Robert ducked into the first one he saw. He sent an encrypted PGP message to Bryce with the location of the dumpster and instructions on how to find the phone. He also advised him to get a taxi off the street to take him there – and not to call one or to take his own car. Robert rode up to the top of Billy Goat Hill where he had a 360-degree view of everything around him, including the dumpster, stashed the bike, and waited.

About 45 minutes later, Robert saw a yellow taxi stop at the dumpster. Bryce exited the vehicle and retrieved the phone. Robert rang him almost immediately.

"You sure you haven't been followed?"

"I don't think so."

"Good. Then come up to the top of the hill."

"Are you kidding? That could kill me!"

"It's not that steep. Go slowly."

The only way to truly be sure that Bryce had not been followed was to watch him as he made his way up the hill. It was a bit of a hike, but he had been advised to take it easy. Robert watched Bryce and all points around the park in his field glasses.

When Bryce reached the top, he was hacking and gasping for breath. He sat on a bench next to Robert, wheezing.

"You're the one who wanted the meeting."

Bryce nodded. "It was for you."

"For me?"

"Yeah. Some hotshot detective from Phoenix thinks the same person did the Phoenix, Atascadero, McDonald's and New York terrorist killings."

"So?"

"So? You don't care? I thought you'd want to know."

Robert shrugged. "It's useful information, but you could have given it to me by PGP."

"I just wanted to make sure you were still in the game."

"You sound like a coach."

"This Phoenix detective, he's a real hound dog, you know? He'll never quit."

Robert brought his field glasses to his eyes and panned the bottom of the hill again.

"He's got to do what he's got to do."

"Just watch your back. And, if I never see you again, I just wanted to say thank you."

"No need. Now, call yourself a taxi with that phone and throw it into that dumpster when you get to the bottom of the hill."

Robert watched Bryce walk away, knowing that he would probably never see him again.

***

Joshua Maynard received a call from Detective DeFasio in New York. It wasn't the news he was hoping for. DeFasio's team had been unable to come up with a possible match on the doctor. With regard to the "Robert Garcia" that Maynard had asked him to check out, there was a death certificate on file for him at City Hall.

"Your guy died in a fire in his apartment in Spanish Harlem about seven months ago."

This surprised Maynard, but didn't shake his resolve. He had gotten excited over leads that had gone cold before. He put Robert's dossier into the inactive pile, along with Jamal Abama's and decided to concentrate on the others.

Halfway through his day, he received a call from Bokowski.

"We've got a positive hit on Garcia out of the Nevada DMV. He's in Vegas!"

Maynard was surprised, but not overly so. Apparently, Robert had come back from the dead.

CHAPTER FORTY

The dog experienced his usual convulsions, together with wailing and crying, to mark Robert's homecoming. When Robert set down his backpack, the dog jumped up on him, with his paws over his shoulders, and licked his face. He pushed him down.

"Okay, okay, I get it, I get it! Now, let's go out."

The dog ran between his legs, almost knocking him down, and out the door into the early morning air. The sun was just starting to rise, but the valley had kept the heat in like a lid on a boiling pot, so it was still very warm. The dog did his business quickly, sniffed around a bit, and then came running back in to enjoy a long-awaited meal. Robert's phone was blinking. It was one of those "antiques" with an old-fashioned built-in answering machine. He pushed the play button.

"Julio, where have you been? It's me. I thought we might catch a movie or something tonight. Anyway, call me."

The machine beeped and then played another message from Virginia.

"Okay, I guess no movie. You must be busy. Call me later."

That was it – the entire display of Robert's social life over a 90-second period – the dog and the girl. Robert didn't have many emotions, but the dog and the girl made him feel like his mother was still alive, and that was good. But, as Bryce had warned him, the heat was on, and it could prove to be hotter than any Las Vegas summer. It was time for Robert to close accounts and disappear.

**

Later that day, Robert went to the mailbox to check the mail. It was something that he did rarely, but it was the only way to open the few bills he had, buy money orders right there at the facility, and send them off. He finished all the business, and, as he made his way back to the parking lot, he heard a voice behind him.

"Julio Ignacio? Robert Garcia?"

Robert turned his head to see two men in suits, who were obviously FBI, and another man who was wearing a lanyard in place of a tie and a cowboy hat, approaching him at a quick pace. He scolded himself for not being aware of them when he pulled up.

"Who's asking?"

"FBI. I'm Special Agent Wokowski and this is Special Agent McHenry. And this is Detective Maynard from the Phoenix Police Department. May we talk to you a moment?"

"You can talk. If I have anything to say, I'll let my lawyer do it."

"You packin', Robert?" The cowboy was sharp, better than the feds.

"I've got my gun right here on my belt. Second Amendment."

"Right. All the same, would you mind giving it to us while we talk?"

"I don't surrender my sidearm to any man, Hoss, but I can put your mind at ease."

Quicker than they could drop their mouths or draw their weapons, and they all tried, Robert popped out his Glock, flipped open the catch, dropped the magazine, opened the chamber and popped out the live round. At that point, the three had their pistols on him. He raised his hands.

"Am I under arrest?"

"You try something like that again and you damn well will be," replied Maynard. Wokowski wiped sweat from his brow with a shaky hand and then asked, "Can we go somewhere to talk?"

"Right here is as good a place as any. Now, why don't you boys put those guns away? You're making me nervous."

They put their guns away and Robert sheathed his weapon.

Wokowski, the sneering little snot, gleefully played with Robert's aliases. "So Mr. Garcia, or should I say Mr. Ignacio, do you know why we'd like to talk to you?"

"Don't know, don't care." Robert spit on the pavement. It was so hot it seemed to sizzle. He leaned against his motorcycle.

"It's about several murders of Muslim extremists. Atascadero, Phoenix, New York."

"Not interested."

"We think you have something to do with them," said McHenry, the normally silent observer. Wokowski glared at him.

"Sounds like this conversation is turning into 'talk to my lawyer.' I don't know anything about any murders."

"There's a burned up body in your old apartment in Spanish Harlem which tells us differently."

"Really? Don't know anything about that either."

"Of course not."

"Is that your case, Wokowski?"

"No, it isn't, but we may have something to offer you to make all your troubles disappear."

"I told you I'm not interested."

"It's a better offer than federal prison."

"If you boys had any evidence against me, I'd be in handcuffs in the back of your car."

Wokowski frowned but he didn't give in. "It comes from high up."

"If you were from the company, I'd be in the trunk of your car."

"Not the CIA, the NCTC."

"Those guys who compile all the data on the terrorists and throw it to you feds so you can fumble the ball and screw up everything like you did in San Bernardino?"

Wokowski's look turned from sarcastic to sour as he ignored the comment. "The director of the NCTC, Nathan

Anderson, wants you to come back to work for the government, doing the same type of jobs you did before."

"No thanks. I'm retired."

"You'd be a free agent, but if you ever got caught, all bets are off."

Maynard was frowning.

"I have a feeling the cowboy's not on the same page as you fellas."

"That's right, I'm not. I think you did the Phoenix murder and I aim to prosecute you for it."

"If I knew what the hell you're talking about, and I don't, I think you need something called evidence. Hunches don't result in too many convictions nowadays."

"What should I tell the director about his offer?"

Robert leaned close to Wokowski. "You tell him he can stick it where the sun don't shine."

"Mr. Garcia, I should remind you that we're the federal government..."

"Yeah, the biggest bunch of crooks there ever was."

"...And if we can catch you this easily, you won't be able to hide again."

"Didn't know I was hiding. Anyway, thanks for the chat."

Robert swung a leg over his bike and started the ignition.

"You'll be hearing from the NYPD about the dead man that was found in your apartment."

"Look forward to it." Robert saluted and took off. Maynard's eyes were trained on him as if they were looking at him through a gunsight. Robert's life was over – again.

187

CHAPTER FORTY ONE

Robert used counter-surveillance measures to make his way back to the apartment. He took a different route, and doubled back several times to assure he was not being tailed before heading to the place that he had called home. Now it was just a place. The dog greeted him on opening the door with the usual fervor. Robert petted him and fed him, and sat at the table and watched for the sixty seconds it took him to eat his food. Then, he took the dog to the kennel. He booked it for three weeks, but gave them an overstuffed wad of cash enough to cover six months.

"Put the rest on my account, in case I'm a little longer."

The surprised clerk looked at the lump of cash like it was a rare moon rock and began counting it into the drawer. Robert got down on his knees and rubbed the dog behind the ears. The dog whined because he knew he was being abandoned yet another time. He had been a great friend to Robert, and Robert knew he would never see him again.

The dog and the girl.

The girl would not be receiving a farewell like the dog. Robert was already gone. That night, he cleared out and wiped down his apartment. He filled up an abandoned shopping cart with his possessions and took them to a nearby dumpster, where he burned them. Then he made his way to the storage unit, where he wiped down his Honda and left it in the locker. It would be a good payoff once they foreclosed on it for the bill. Robert hopped on the 990 and drove away from the dog, the girl, Las Vegas, and the life of Julio Ignacio.

CHAPTER FORTY TWO

Robert had to put some mileage between himself and Las Vegas before deciding where to make his next base camp. This time, it had to be somewhere he didn't need to worry about licenses or registrations, girls or dogs. He headed to Denver, knowing he could get lost in the crowd while he was looking for a more secluded place to light. He was tired when he arrived in town, so he cruised around looking for a place to rest where he could remain anonymous. He found it with the Jacaro Motel on Colorado Boulevard.

The Jacaro Motel was right out of the 1950s. Although it looked like it had never been remodeled since then, Robert could see that a few coats of paint had been splashed on the walls over the years. Robert signed the register as "Ben Frank" and when the clerk asked for his ID, he handed him a stack of hundreds.

"That's my ID. This is for the room." Robert shoved another hundred over the desk. The clerk took the hint and pocketed the wad, smiled with hospitality, and slid his key to him.

"Welcome to the Jacaro, Mr. Frank."

Robert nodded and snatched the key. He then began his research project on his computer. This time it was not to identify his new target but to locate a place to live that was remote enough not to have neighbors and close enough to the city to not be noticed coming and going for supplies.

Robert finally found the area he was looking for: A secluded forest community with mostly vacation cabins. People who did happen to live there would be less likely to be alarmed by seeing an unfamiliar face because the cabins in the area were mostly for rent. Robert couldn't rent one over the Internet, so he called a couple of numbers and arranged to meet the owners of two different cabins. He took a ride out to Pine, Colorado to check them out. It was only an hour's drive from the big city but a world away, nestled against the base of the Rocky Mountains. The area also was not mapped for GPS navigation systems, and registered as "off-road" to them, another plus for Robert.

At the second cabin he visited, Robert was lucky to find Rocky Melville, the owner, an Army vet who had actually lived in his cabin from time to time. He was an old school old- timer who didn't have a smartphone and thought the Internet was some kind of fishing appliance, although he did offer free WiFi, which Robert, of course, would never use. He would hack into a different neighbor's system if ever the need arose.

Rocky's wrinkled eyes widened when Robert offered to pay him cash for six months in advance, and he smiled with his lips to cover a bottom row of rotting teeth. He told Robert a sob story about the IRS and how every time he took a charge card or check, he had to whip the money out of his checking account right quick or they would take it. The cabin was in his dead sister's name, but he had never transferred the title to himself because he didn't want the government to get it. The rental agreement between Rocky and Robert was a handshake.

"I'll take it."

"Great! Now let me show you some of the benefits."

Rocky led Robert outside to the storage shed and unlocked and opened the door. Inside was a hodge-podge of clutter, typical of a hoarder, with piles of moldy magazines on the floor, a collection of hats hung on a rack against the wall, heads of deer and dozens of sets of antlers, and an assortment of fishing poles.

"Are you a fisherman, Sam?"

Robert had a half-second delayed reaction upon hearing his new pseudonym for the first time.

"Oh, yeah, I do like to fish."

Rocky proudly motioned to a corner of assorted fishing gear. "Here I've got all of my fishing equipment, which you're welcome to use at any time."

"Much obliged."

There was not one but at least six tackle boxes overflowing with gear and about twenty spools of fishing line of various sizes.

"There's a lot of good fishing in the creeks and streams around here. That trout's awful tasty. Once you have it, you won't want to eat anything else. And the Pine River's got some great fly fishing. You ever done any fly fishing?"

"No."

Rocky opened a case gleaming with shiny flies, almost alive with their fringes and shredded feathers in fiery oranges, blood reds, cobalt blues, iridescent violets and cornhusk yellows.

"Patience. That's the key. You have enough patience and the big ones will always come to you."

Robert nodded and the old man directed him back inside.

"Do any hunting, Sam?"

Robert grinned. "All my life."

"Then let me show you something really special."

Under a stag head in the living room above the fireplace was a rifle in a glass case. Rocky fished in his pocket, withdrew the key, opened the case and lifted out the rifle. He held it like a baby in his hands as he presented it to Robert carefully.

"This is a mighty fine rifle, Sam. Put that big one up there down. I keep most of the trophies in the shed because they're not for most people, but this one was special. I remember the time I bagged him. He was a beauty, that one, and put many a good steak on the table."

Robert took the gun gently from Rocky. It was a lovely Mannlicher-Schoenauer, an Australian-made deer rifle. He held it up to his cheek and looked through the sight out the window.

"That Mannlicher's a beauty. Since I know you're a real hunting man, you're welcome to use it at your leisure."

"Thanks, Rocky. I'll take good care of it."

"I know you will." Rocky handed him the key and walked outside with Robert. Rocky held up his finger.

"I didn't show you the garage."

Rocky walked over to the garage and unlocked the door. Like the shed, it was overstuffed with useless treasures, but also had an old 70s style Ford Ranger pickup in the middle of all that clutter.

"Noticed you had just a motorbike. Well this baby is good for small trips to town to pick up supplies. It's all registered and insured. You can use it when you need to go pick up your staples."

The last of the keys, which belonged to the pickup, was placed into Robert's open palm.

After Rocky had left, Robert paced the property and its surroundings to get a lay of the land. It was a rustic cabin with a wood burning fireplace and a propane-powered kitchen and plenty of property separated it from the neighboring structures. Rocky told him the fishing was good in the mountain area surrounding the cabin which gave Robert the notion of living off the land. If he could do that it would minimize his appearances in public. It was a stone's throw to a thick clump of trees which marked the beginning of the forest, with several trails running into it.

Robert took the pickup back to Denver to fetch supplies. He couldn't risk being seen in any smaller towns closer to the cabin. He picked up some ammo for the rifle in a sporting goods store, along with some extra hunting gear and a few fishing items (even though Rocky had too many). Then he shopped in a 24-hour discount grocery store to stock the cabin with enough staples to last the season. Robert headed back to Pine, stopping only on the way for a burger. With luck (and some skill), he would not have to make too many more return trips.

As Robert settled into his new cabin abode, it was dark, cold and quiet. He had been in less favorable conditions – sliding in the mud into a foxhole with mortars and shells exploding overhead, for example – but he had never experienced an existence that was this quiet before. Inside was only the creaking of the floorboards of the musty cabin, outside the faint buzzing sound of night insects. There was nobody here to bother him – no dog asking for food or to go out or to be caressed. No girl bugging him on the phone. Robert never had a problem being alone, but, for the first time in years, he felt lonely.

The cabin was dark and chilly. Instead of peace, all Robert found was inquietude. Every creak of the settling of the cabin and every brush of the wind outside had him pulling out his gun and creeping up to the window to look outside through the corner of it. He went to the bathroom to dress his wound, sliding off the sticky old gauze, cleaning the injury over the sink with alcohol and patching it up with new material. That kept Robert busy for less than half an hour before that unsettling feeling came back.

Robert lay in bed and stared at the large, cracked redwood beams in the ceiling. He loosened his grip on the Glock and put it under the pillow next to his head. It looked to be a long night.

CHAPTER FORTY THREE

Nathan Anderson squirmed in his chair. He slammed down his pen and regarded Wokowski and Samuels with incredulity.

"What do you mean: you lost him?"

"We lost him, sir. He just, well, he vanished."

"Well, why didn't you arrest him?"

Wokowski looked down at the floor and then back up at Anderson defiantly.

"No warrant, no indictment, he wasn't fleeing the scene of any crime – there was nothing we could have arrested him for."

"And did you communicate my offer?"

Wokowski looked away. "Yes, we did."

"What did he say?"

With a frown and a grin of embarrassment, Wokowski answered, "He said you could stick your offer where the sun don't shine, sir."

Anderson's lips puckered as he frowned with disgust. "Then we have to neutralize him."

"Sir, we can't kill him."

"That's not what I meant, Wokowski. I meant he's got to be taken off the streets, with a warrant, without a warrant. I don't care how you get him, just get him and figure out a way to make it stick so he's not out there going around killing people."

"It's not that simple, sir."

"That's why we have the FBI, the best law enforcement institution in the world. Let's get it done, gentlemen."

Anderson stood and the two agents got the idea. They got up and left his office.

Out of hearing distance of the office, Wokowski said, "He sounds like a football coach."

"Yeah, with no playbook."

Wokowski and Samuels discussed the dilemma and decided it would be best solved by their "real" boss, Bill Carpenter. Two agents from Washington didn't have the capacity to put a dragnet over the city of Las Vegas, if Paladine was even still there. They were going to need a bigger force.

***

A shrill, inhuman shriek sound startled Robert out of his sleep. He tried to reach for his gun, but he was paralyzed.

The shadow of an approaching figure danced in the moon-lit corridor. Robert tried to move again, but he couldn't. He tried to roll out of the bed but he remained stationary. The figure was getting closer and Robert could hear the sound of breathing as the shadows grew taller and moved into the room. Then it was clear who the intruder was. Standing in the doorway was an ISIS jihadist, holding a scimitar. He ginned deviously as he approached the bed, and raised his weapon above Robert's neck.

Robert opened his eyes, grabbed his gun and was on his feet in less than a second after waking. He rotated on his feet as an axis, doing a 360-degree spin of the room with his Glock, then went to the window, peeled open the blinds and looked out. Dawn was breaking and he had made it through the first night alive.

CHAPTER FORTY FOUR

The phone rang, breaking Joshua Maynard's concentration. He picked it up, angrily and impatiently.

"Yes?"

"Josh, where are you?"

It was the shrill voice of Joshua's ex-wife, Cynthia. She always had a way about her and that way usually rubbed Joshua the wrong way, especially when she was in "crisis mode," which was often.

"I'm at home, working on a case."

"Josh, it's Saturday and you're thirty minutes late to pick up the kids!"

"Oh, God, I'm sorry. I'm coming now."

"Save it! I'll drop them at my mother's."

Josh could feel her seething over the phone.

"No, no, I'm coming, I'm coming."

It was a cold reception at the ex-house of Joshua Maynard. Not from Erica and Jim, who were always happy to see him, but from Cynthia, who stayed back and let her new husband, Ken, take care of the transfer. In Ken, Cynthia had found everything that lacked in Joshua – a man who was so attentive, he sacrificed his own masculinity just to please her every whim. But he was a good stepfather to the kids, so Joshua couldn't complain – well, maybe too good.

Five-year-old Erica jumped into the arms of her father, while seven-year-old Jim hung his head. He loved his dad, but was going to miss hanging out with the neighborhood boys this weekend. They had planned a street baseball game and he was supposed to play first base.

Erica was bubbling with conversation, while Josh tried to pull it out of Jim with a series of questions like, "How's it going at school?" that were met with one syllable answers like "fine." In contrast to Erica's diarrhea of the mouth, Jim's monotone answers told Josh just where he stood with his son. When he and Cynthia were together, he was a great father and a bad husband. Without her he was just a terrible father.

Maynard didn't have any plans for the kids, so he took them back to his house, turned on the television and went back to work. The guilt hung like a shadow over his shoulder as he sat at his computer, answering questions from time to time from the kids, but he soon drifted back into a workaholic state as he surfed the latest data on Paladine.

***

As the days turned to weeks and the weeks to months, Robert almost lost track of the sunrises and sunsets. He was trying to live the life of a hermit, but it wasn't working well for him. He cast his line into the stream and kicked back on the soft pad of pine needles against a redwood tree. He didn't quite have the hang of fly fishing, so he decided to start the old fashioned way. He had dozed off to the music of chirping birds for about half an hour when he felt a pull on his line and tightened his grip on the pole. He jerked his wrist and reeled as the fish fought against his efforts, bending and stretching his pole to the breaking point. Finally, the fish lost and Robert swung it into his net. He set it on the floor of the forest, wrenched the hook out of its mouth and watched it flop about. The fish was a beautiful green rainbow trout with a shiny orange tint and black spots. He kept at it for another two hours, until he had added four more fish to his quota.

The countryside was so quiet you could almost hear your own thoughts echoing in your skull. Robert cleaned and dressed the fish, one for dinner and four for freezing. The lull after this work left his hands idle and he was impatient and jittery. It was too dark to take Rocky's deer gun out for a hunt, so he paced the cabin like a ping pong ball bouncing against the walls.

Robert took the bike out for a ride. Once he was on the open road, his anxiety level dropped a bit. He realized then that he needed to get back to work – the sooner the better.

***

The investigation on Garcia had dried up and the passage of time was making it less likely it would come to a satisfactory conclusion. Wokowski and Samuels had "lost track" of Robert somehow. The game was at a stalemate. Maynard would just have to wait for Paladine's next move. He tapped his index finger against the screen of his monitor.

"I'm gonna get you, Paladine. It's just a matter of time."

"Who you talking to, daddy?"

The miniature voice came from the corridor. "Nobody, sweetheart. Daddy's just working." He beckoned to Erica

203

with a sweep of his hand and she ran and jumped onto his lap and cuddled up against his chest. She looked up at Joshua with a sad, puckered face.

"You're always working, daddy."

Joshua gazed at his daughter as the guilt pangs ran up his spine.

"I know, baby, I'm sorry. Tomorrow, we'll have a lot of fun, okay?"

"Okay, daddy." She put her thumb in her mouth and, in just a few minutes, fell asleep.

CHAPTER FORTY FIVE

Wokowski and Samuels had their meeting with Bill Carpenter, but Carpenter was not pleased. He was not going to be responsible for the screw-ups of Nathan Anderson or even his own agents. But he did assure them they would get all the support they needed. Whether they had to get every agent of every office in Nevada on it, this Paladine would be found.

Like a pack of bloodhounds, led by Wokowski and Samuels, federal agents in Las Vegas proceeded to turn over every rock and leaf in search of the terrorist killer. They put out an all-points bulletin on Julio Ignacio and the motorcycle registered in his name but came up with nothing. Every known confidential informant was grilled. Wokowski and Samuels interrogated the clerks at Robert's remote mailbox, but they didn't know anything. Then, they paid a visit to the DMV.

Wokowski and Samuels split up and spoke to every clerk in the office, showing them each a picture of Robert. Finally, Samuels showed the picture to a clerk named Virginia Linder, whose eyes flung wide open in astonishment.

"Why are you looking for Julio?"

Samuels fired back with his federal double-talk. "I'm not at liberty to discuss it, ma'am. Do you know this man?"

"Well, yes. He's my..."

"Your what?"

"He's my friend. What has he done?"

"Again, ma'am, I'm not at liberty to discuss it. Let's just say he's a person of interest we need to talk to."

Samuels motioned to Wokowski, who came over. Virginia closed her window and led them into the break room so they could discuss it with her further.

Once they had all sat down in the plastic chairs around the circular table that was next to the coffee machine and water cooler, the agents started in on her again.

"Wait a minute! You haven't told me yet. Is Julio in any kind of trouble?"

"Well, yes, ma'am, we think he may be, but all we're trying to do now is talk to him. Do you know how we might find him?"

"Julio doesn't have a cell phone, but I've got his phone number."

"Can you give it to us please, ma'am?"

Virginia gave them Robert's phone number, explained that she hadn't known him long and knew he lived in an apartment in Las Vegas but she didn't know where. She told them that he had a dog, too. The interrogation went on for two hours, until they were satisfied that they had milked enough information from her and she could be released.

The FBI tracked the actual telephone number through the records of the phone company to Robert's apartment, obtained a quick search warrant, and broke into it. It was as empty as if nobody had ever lived there. They spoke to the manager, who gave the same story about Robert and his dog that Virginia had given, and described Robert and his motorcycle. An artist did a sketch of Robert from the descriptions given by Virginia and the manager and it went out over the wire, along with the photo from his DMV file. It was a nondescript drawing and an ambiguous photograph, either one of which could have passed for many different people. The fact was that Robert did not have any outward physical traits that anybody would have considered to be unique.

***

Robert was getting antsy. He donned his hunting gear and took the hunting rifle out, thinking that would blow off some steam. As Robert adeptly snuck through the woods in search of deer or elk, he found some droppings in a clearing by a stream and found a place to cache himself. He patiently waited and, finally, a grand-looking elk appeared in the clearing. Robert aimed, fired, and took the beautiful creature down in one shot. He dragged the body down the trail to the side of the road and went to fetch the truck so he could take his prize home and prepare the meat, a task which took the rest of the day.

But it seemed the work couldn't stay away from Robert, or he couldn't stay away from it. He delved back into the dungeons of the Darknet, mastering his many puppet jihadist aliases, looking for an open door to this grand terrorist scheme he had read about in Jahawi's computer. Since he knew virtually all of the lieutenants of ISIS in the states, he knew exactly which digital doors to knock on.

Robert offered up his services to Allah under the well-established but artificial history of his namesake, Malik Abdul, a respected warrior who was a legendary commando and freedom fighter in the Middle East. He expressed a desire, as he had for months and months, to go to Syria and join the fight. Finally, he was invited by PGP message to communicate with one of the assistants for Badi Hasib Najjar, second in command at ISIS whom was thought to be in Al-Raqqah, the self-proclaimed capital of the Islamic State. Robert met him in a designated chat room with a password-protected entrance which used TorChat, an encrypted instant messaging system.

"Peace be with you, brother."

"And with you."

"Your reputation precedes you."

"I am but a servant of Allah."

"Allhamdulillah."

"Yes, brother, Allah Akbar."

"The caliph himself asks for your help."

"I live to serve him."

"But you must understand the need for discretion."

"Of course. The Kafir are watching."

"Yes, and that is why you must be tested if you are to be in His service."

Robert was instructed to meet his compatriot in a secluded area of the Hudson River Valley. Robert knew this would be a test, but he had been through more rigorous examinations.

***

Nathan Anderson gulped his coffee impatiently as he pored through the analysts' reports. Something big was brewing in the virtual caliphate, but nobody had a clue what it could be. All of the operations by undercover agents who had been sent to penetrate ISIS's online stronghold had resulted in nothing but a string of arrests of small-time wannabe jihadists who had pledged to take out infidels or go to war against them in Syria. Nathan's frustration internalized to the point where it was giving him palpitations. If only he had the power to send his own analysts in undercover, maybe he could obtain some useful information to wage the war against terror.

The president took his briefings of inactivity as if everything was fine. He passed off Nathan's hunch that something big was brewing as over-enthusiasm. After all, this was the Jaycee Team. Targeted drone killings were working and were eliminating head ISIS figures, never mind the women and children as collateral damage. The Commander-in-Chief downplayed Anderson's concerns for heightening the alert level around airports and major institutions. He didn't want to panic the people, nor did he want to get a reputation as the "president who cried wolf" by painting an orange or red alert every time ISIS waved their black flag.

The briefings from Wokowski and Samuels had shed little light on the subject. They, too, had surmised that something was brewing. The social media sites were ablaze with well-wishers and warriors, waving Islamic State flags and spouting energetic jihadist rhetoric. To them, Anderson's hunch was "right on."

"But what do you think we should do, sir?"

"I think we should go deep undercover and try to infiltrate them."

"For that we need someone who is fluent in Arabic, who can pass their vetting process and convince them they can be trusted."

Like Paladine, thought Anderson.

"You have any candidates in mind?"

"We do, sir. We'll have to clear it with Director Carpenter, though."

"Of course."

Anderson looked back down at his reports. As the agents were leaving the room, he raised his head.

"Anything on the Paladine case?"

"No, sir, that's a dead end. Our Las Vegas dragnet stopped cold, so we figure he's left town. And he's been quiet for a while."

CHAPTER FORTY SIX

The preparations for Robert's road trip were minimal – no dog to feed, no mail to check   just pack his bag, lock the door to the cabin and jump on the bike. As he motored from the Rocky Mountains he turned a switch in his mind. From that point on, he would speak only Arabic and think only in Arabic. He wiggled back into the skin of Malik Abdul, the fabled warrior of the Iraqi insurgency, whose reputation had been built by millions of dollars of perception management of the media by the CIA. Through the Midwest he ran over the backstory of Malik in his mind and became the holy soldier for Allah they would expect to see. Finally, he reached the rendezvous point in Upstate New York. He stashed his bike and hitchhiked to the designated location not too far from the Bear Mountain Bridge and waited.

Robert was picked up by a white van with no windows, which was probably originally designed to be a delivery van. In this case, it would deliver Robert to a location his future handlers obviously didn't want him to know. To greet him, a dark-skinned, bearded jihadi exited the passenger side door and stood before him. Robert could sense the speculation in his eyes as the man hailed him with the Arabic phrase, "Peace be with you."

"As-salaam 'alaykum."

Robert took the man's extended hand and responded, "Wa 'alaykum salaam."

The man slid open the side door of the van and directed Robert to get in. He found a seat inside, which was filled with five other men, whom he greeted as well. Between the body of the van and the driver's cab was a partition with a small, tinted glass window, which was presently shut. Its cargo loaded, the truck took off for its eventual destination.

Robert kept track of time, but could only speculate where they were headed, whether it was Albany, Syracuse, or maybe Buffalo, because there was no way for them to look out. The men in the van were short on conversation. They didn't reveal much about themselves and Robert didn't care. After over three hours, he speculated they must be in some remote, rural area near the Adirondack Mountains.

Finally the car came to a stop and the side door slid open. They were ordered out of the van, military style, by the man who had greeted Robert, and instructed to line up. Robert stood at attention in front of the man as another man approached. He was of average height, shortened hair, and had a long scar that protruded from above his right cheekbone into the thick dark brown hairs of his beard. Robert recognized this must be Badi Hasib Najjar. He was to be vetted by one of the chiefs at the very top echelon of the Islamic State.

It soon became clear to Robert that he was at a terrorist training compound, smack in the middle of Americana, teaching their jihadist mantra of kill the infidels and training how to shoot them, thanks to the umbrella of the First and Second Amendments to the United States Constitution. He suppressed and filed away his anger toward these cretins, resisted the urge to turn the weapon they had given him on all of them, and crawled back into his jihadi persona.

The tests may have been grueling for some, but they were child's play for Robert. He began with a string of recruits in a traditional indoor shooting range with a CZ-75 SP-01 9mm handgun. Robert donned earplugs, took a shooting stance and fired six rounds at the target at about 50 meters. He pushed a button, and the half-man sized target sped toward him on a cable. It had three perfect holes in the head and three perfect holes in the bullseye area of the chest. Robert replaced the target and set it away at 100 meters. He fired another six rounds, three again spot-on in the head and three in the chest.

The man who had met Robert at the van, who still remained nameless, collected the targets. He paused, held up Robert's, one after the other, and harrumphed before moving on to the next shooter.

Robert and the others were herded outside to an outdoor shooting range and each outfitted with an AK-47. Robert had handled this gun thousands of times and held it like it had always been a part of his body. He shot the targets at the maximum distance of 1,500 meters. After making adjustments for wind factor and the weapon's own particulars, he hit them with extreme precision. Then, they were put through an obstacle course. He crawled on his belly through sand and mud with live rounds shooting over his head, scaled walls and climbed rope with his weapon strung over his shoulder, and emerged from the course before anyone else.

Next, Robert entered a large kill house. As he navigated the massive rooms, life-sized mannequins confronted him with varying degrees of threats. He had done this many times while he was in the service, hitting only the "bad guys." This time, Robert had to change his thinking. He flew through the kill house, but this time the "bad guys" he shot were the law enforcement officers and unarmed infidels. He left the jihadist "good guys" unharmed.

From the thinning crowd of his peers, it was evident to Robert that the vetting process had already begun, and that he was part of a final group who would be put to the next test. When he was sequestered in a dark room that contained an empty chair and what Robert surmised was a two-way mirror, Robert figured that, since he had passed the arms and physical prowess tests, this would be an examination of his loyalty.

Through a speaker in the ceiling, Robert listened to and responded to questions about his family history, his background, military and insurgency experience. After two hours of interrogation, he was taken to an area where he took a seat on one of two sofas, was offered black or mint tea or cardamom coffee, and opted for the coffee. A woman completely covered in a hajib entered and placed a tray with two cups of coffee on it, and Robert helped himself to one of them. As he sipped, the man with the scar on his face entered and Robert rose to his feet.

"As-salaam 'alaykum."

"Wa 'alaykum salaam."

He took Robert's hand in a firm shake.

"Please, sit."

Robert lowered himself back onto the couch as the scar-faced man sat.

"Do you know who I am?"

"Yes, Badi Hasib Najjar. You are a great and faithful warrior of God."

"And you are Malik Abdul, a warrior of the Iraqi insurgency. Whatever brought you to America?"

"I am but a humble servant of God and do not boast of my exploits. I have answered the call of the caliphate to wage war on the infidels in their own homes but I fear that my victories acting alone have been too few."

Najjar took a sip of his mint tea and smiled. "We have plans for you, brother."

"What plans?"

"An operation."

"When will I be told?"

He paused, sniffing the steam from the tea and then taking another mouthful.

"Are you prepared to sacrifice yourself for God?"

"Yes, I am."

"Then you will be told at the appropriate time. I think you must realize that we will be using your particular skills."

"I am happy to use them and will die for the better good."

"You are a good soldier, Malik. I have a feeling you will serve God for many more years on earth, Inshallah."

Najjar set his cup down on the saucer and rose. The door to the room opened and two men appeared. Robert stood and shook his hand, then Najjar took his leave. Robert was left in the room for about thirty minutes, then met at the door by the handler who had greeted him at the beginning of his journey.

"It is finished, Malik, and welcome to the caliph's colonial army. I am Colonel Fahad Qurashi."

This time, when Qurashi shook Robert's hand, he also double-kissed him on the cheeks, a sign that Robert was now part of the family.

CHAPTER FORTY SEVEN

Even though Joshua Maynard had hit a dead end in his investigation and the mysterious suspect, Robert Garcia, seemed to have vanished from the face of the earth, the hype on Paladine had only increased. His son was even asking him to buy him a Paladine action figure for his birthday. Maynard was sickened by the idea of vigilantism, which was becoming popular on every social media site. Even in the playgrounds at school, the kids were playing "Paladine games." Instead of the old cowboys and Indians that Maynard had played in his childhood, his children were jumping out from behind structures in the play yard, spraying Muslim jihadists with make-believe machine gun fire.

Joshua had gone through all the evidence over and over. His captain told him he had been spending too much time on the case and it was affecting his workload. As a result, he did more unscheduled and unpaid overtime, working the dead case at night. He put his elbows on his desk and buried his face in his hands. There had to be a break in this case soon. He couldn't bear to consider it unsolved when they had already come so far.

Joshua Maynard was haunted by Robert Garcia. Suspects had evaded him before, but this was the first time that no trace had been left behind. Usually there was something to follow or some remnant of the old life that drew the suspect back – a family member or a girlfriend. When Joshua learned that Robert owned a dog, he had a hunch this would be the magnet that would draw Robert back to his old life.

Joshua had checked all the dog kennels in Las Vegas until he found one where the owner had apparently abandoned the dog, but left a large deposit to cover an extended stay – in cash. Joshua questioned the manager of the kennel about the dog's fate.

"Can I see the dog?"

"Sure."

The manager led Joshua to the kennels, where he was introduced to a big, dumb looking mutt with droopy ears. Joshua knelt in front of the cage and talked to him.

"Hey, boy. Where's your owner?"

The dog reacted by wagging his tail and whining. Joshua stood up and addressed the manager.

"What happens if the owner doesn't claim the dog when the deposit runs out?'

"Well, we wait the required time and then we take the dog to the pound."

Joshua thought a moment. "In addition to telling me if the owner comes back for him, please keep my card in case he never comes back. In that case, I'll take the dog."

The manager looked at Joshua in surprise, then nodded and smiled. "Will do."

Robert went back to his alter-ego life of a mountain hermit, but retained the Malik persona. He thought and dreamed only in Arabic. He surfed the Net of the caliphate religiously, searching for his call to action on a daily basis. There was no gym in the outback, but he worked out, running in the forest and doing hundreds of pull-ups from the branches of trees. He practiced his shooting in remote parts of the forest, both with his handgun and the hunting rifle, putting himself through his own basic training routine. Day by day, Robert roughed it like a survivalist, fishing and living off venison meat and edible forest plants. At night he surfed the caliphate's pages and chat rooms.

Finally, Robert received the call. He was to be at the same meeting point as before in exactly four days.

***

This time, Robert stayed at the same training camp for three weeks. Each day consisted of basic training, broken up only for prayers. Robert trained with about twenty other men and was given the rank of captain and put in charge of his own squad of seven, all expert marksmen. Robert didn't recognize any of them, but he knew from observing them in training that they all had extensive military experience. He also knew from observation that, unlike him, they all believed in God and that what they were doing was His will. He vowed then and there that none of them would be allowed to live. Robert had served his country and done unspeakable things in its name. If it was going to be "us" or "them" then Robert would make sure the "us" side would live and take as many of "them" down as he could.

Life in the camp was military style. As an officer, Robert had his own meager quarters but the men bunked together on cots in a common cabin. There was no contact with the outside world allowed or even possible and communication with each other was restricted to discussion of the training program. Robert had to feign prayer, which was perhaps the most difficult thing for him to act out. Five times a day, he lay out his prayer mat facing Mecca, prostate, with his forehead to the ground, and pretended to praise the glory of God and ask his forgiveness. Robert no longer believed in any God. His faith lay only in his own abilities. Since all his activities were monitored, arms were stored in high-security lockup, and the camp had the security of a prison, there would be no sneaking away, no surprise attack from the outside. Robert would have to make his move during the operation itself.

During the second week, the officers were all assembled for a meeting with Badi Hasib Najjar. Finally, the great plans were revealed. In the briefing room, Najjar showed projected satellite and drone surveillance photos of the Indian Point nuclear power plant in New York. Only about 40 miles from New York City, causing a meltdown of any of the three reactors at Indian Point would contaminate everything within a 50-80 mile radius, if the Fukushima experience was any indication. That meant Long Island, Manhattan, and a good chunk of New Jersey, Pennsylvania and Connecticut, just to name a few. A disaster of this proportion would cripple the US economy and bring the infidels to their knees.

Najjar had done all the strategic planning, and showed the officers where their squads would be placed for a commando style attack which would take out the vital equipment serving all three reactors, sabotage spent fuel pools and eliminate personnel, which should result in a complete meltdown of the two active reactors and a fatal nuclear fallout which would kill thousands of non-believers.

Despite the pathetic attempts of the Nuclear Regulatory Commission to prepare nuclear power plants with "force on force" exercises, those drills occurred only every three years and the security teams at the plants were no match for these highly trained commandos. The only thing that was not disclosed was timing. All Najjar said in that respect was that "God will call us to action."

For the next week, they trained in three teams of seven – one commander in charge of six men. Each were equipped with an AK-47, a 9mm handgun with noise and flash suppression, hand grenades, rocket-propelled grenades, C-4 explosives, gas masks, and flak jackets. Najjar was wise. Each team had their own responsibilities, but he trained every team how to take over the others' jobs. This was called redundant training which was paramount to accomplishing the mission. If any team failed for any reason, the others could take over and complete the operation.

Team One, headed by Adwan Badat, an Egyptian with dark, wild eyes, was given the task of establishing a perimeter and taking out the guards, which was the first step of the operation. Team Two, Robert's team, was to breach the facility, gas the occupants, and then destroy the cooling systems for the Indian Point reactor 2. Team Two was to take out the systems for Indian Point reactor 3. Their collective work would cause an unstoppable meltdown of both active reactors. Team Three, under the helm of Nasser Meziani, an Algerian, was to approach from the Hudson River side, commandeer a security boat, take out the rest of the water security team and then blow up the two spent fuel pools, which would cause a massive escape of radioactive material.

Najjar struck Robert as more of a politician than a holy warrior. Even his Islam was political, although he didn't hesitate to exploit the enthusiasm of his comrades. He didn't seem to have the fanaticism of his contemporaries, and Robert had the impression that he must have been a Special Forces officer in Iraq or Syria before the Civil War. In Arabic, Hasib meant "noble" and Najjar meant "carpenter." He wasn't sure if that was Najjar's birth name or a nom de guerre. He saw ambition in Najjar, an aspiration to make the Islamic State the most powerful in the modern world. Robert had seen many such "leaders" during his lifetime – men who had no problem sending others to their deaths for their own gain. He knew at that moment that Najjar must not be allowed to live.

CHAPTER FORTY EIGHT

On a crisp, cool fall morning in Upstate New York, Allah called his warriors to action. The three squads moved out in three vans, with a fourth carrying the commanders, for the four-hour drive to Indian Point. Toward the end of the drive, Qurashi left the command van and joined the others. Najjar's van then sped off to a location that had not been disclosed to any of them. Robert was sure that he would stay close so as not to miss any of the action, but far enough away not to risk being caught. Robert thought of the pleasure it would be to send Najjar to meet his 77 virgins.

When they arrived, the first van calmly stopped at the security checkpoint with the two others behind it. When the guard asked the driver his business, the driver responded by shooting him, and the side door of the van opened with an explosion of automatic fire which killed all the guards at the security checkpoint. The vans smashed through the chain link gates. Team One's van stopped at the administration building. Two men breached the building, shot the four security guards stationed to protect it,, donned their gas masks and threw down the gas canisters. They stormed the security control room, while the other four took sniper positions in a perimeter around the power plant complex. On Colonel Fahad Qurashi's command, they started picking off the guards one by one, and blew up a security Humvee with specially formed RPG in a spectacular explosion.

Robert's team was supposed to take out the second tier of security and then, simultaneously with the assault called by Qurashi, kill the remaining security guards on patrol and smash into the reactor containment buildings, but they never got that far. He commanded them to march double-time and set up a perimeter around the second security checkpoint. As they moved out, Robert shot the first three in the back of the head and the last two to turn around were shot in the face. Robert split from them immediately and disappeared.

"Captain Abdul – Malik – where are you?"

Hearing no response, Qurashi ordered Team One to the reactors. As they moved out, Robert picked them off one by one from his vantage point, and then breached the chain link security perimeters himself and headed waterside. Robert took some small arms fire from two security guards who had sequestered themselves behind concrete barriers. He threw two grenades behind their barriers, which killed both of them, and kept moving. The guards were standing between Robert and the accomplishment of his mission. They were collateral damage.

Robert reached the river with no resistance just in time to see Team Three unloading and heading toward the spent fuel pools. It was too late to blow up the boat because they were already out of it, and he thought he may need it to make his own getaway, so he silently stalked the team and picked off two of them with shots to the head. The other five took cover positions to engage Robert, but they couldn't tell where the fatal shots had come from. They had spread out, so Robert picked up an extra RPG-7 grenade launcher from one of the jihadists he had killed, shot it at the two in the middle and, as the other three ran for cover, he eliminated them with automatic fire from his AK-47.

The reactors and spent fuel pools now secure, Robert doubled back to the boat to make his getaway. As he did, he could hear the alarms of the facility finally sounding off. That meant the police were on their way.

Robert swung his equipment over into the boat and leapt into it. He started it and began to power away, when he heard small arms fire coming from the shore. Robert fired back as he punched the accelerator lever for the boat to its maximum, churning up a plume of whitewater in its exit path.

When Robert had almost reached the opposite shore, he could see the New York Naval Militia boat in pursuit. He turned his craft around, pointed it at the pursuing craft to create a diversion for his escape. Robert jammed the accelerator and dived off the back unseen, hoping that his pursuers would assume he was still onboard. As the militia cruiser fired on Robert's boat, he swam to shore, crossed the road and disappeared in to the forest. He found the van that had been stashed in the forest and opened the unlocked door. The keys were under the visor, as he knew they would be from countless training sessions. He started the van, navigated a small dirt access road and took off up Highway 20, passing oncoming police cars and fire trucks with their lights and sirens blazing.

On this side of the river, Robert's ride was at least half an hour away, and if he couldn't get to it he would have to abandon it. He had no money besides the cash he had stashed on the bike and couldn't risk making a cross-country trip in the third white van, so if he couldn't get back to his bike, he would put as many miles as he could between him and the plant and then steal a motorcycle to complete the short part of his getaway. He would likely need to repeat that scenario several times on his way back to Colorado.

CHAPTER FORTY NINE

While Robert was speeding away, Colonel Qurashi had barricaded himself in the administration building and was facing an invading unit of the New York State Police SWAT team. A van load of them had pulled up to the admin building and another two at the reactor site. The police had set up a command center in the parking lot of the administration building and ordered the first unit to storm it. Qurashi didn't have a chance. He didn't give himself an opportunity to surrender either, and went down with guns blazing. The SWAT team went from floor to floor, securing each room. When they finally found Qurashi on the roof of the building, they wasted no time in firing on him. There would be no more casualties, no chance for surrender. Quarashi attempted to fling a grenade at them, but his body danced like a marionette as it was shredded by the SWAT team's bullets. The grenade, minus the pin which had already been pulled, fell to the ground and Quarashi's body crashed down upon it, absorbing the explosion, but Qurashi never felt it. He was already in Jahannam.

Most of the action was taking place on the other side of the river, so Robert continued his journey through Bear Mountain State Park unperturbed. When he finally reached the other side of the Bear Mountain Bridge, he pulled the van off the road and to the Hessian Lake. Once at the lake, he placed the car in neutral, loaded down the accelerator pedal with some of the heavy equipment and then shoved the transmission into drive. The van propelled itself into the water and it took about three minutes for it to become completely submerged.

Robert completed the rest of the trip on foot. He located the hiding place where he had stashed his bike, unlocked it and began to roll it out when he was struck on the back from behind.

Robert lost his balance and fell to the ground as the pain singed his spine. He struggled on his knees to get back on his feet and looked up at Najjar, who was red in the face with anger and spittle came out with his words.

"Yes, traitor pig, stand up and die like a man!"

Najjar was holding a two-by-four, and swung at Robert's head. Robert dodged the swing but the next one connected. Najjar had aimed for his solar plexus, but Robert arched backwards and took the blow in his stomach. He gasped for air as he stumbled.

"You destroyed my operation! Months of planning and organization!"

He swung again, hitting Robert's leg and knocking him to the ground and, once again, Robert stood up, sizing him up, waiting for an opportunity to strike back. Najjar was furious, which was the only weakness Robert could find to exploit at the time. Robert had learned all too well that there was no place for emotion in business, and anger was like panic – neither had its place in a fight.

"You should have used a gun, Najjar."

"That would have spared you the painful death you are about to receive."

Robert charged Najjar, knocking him in the mid-section with his head as Najjar delivered another blow to his hip. Najjar recovered his balance and smashed Robert in the ribs, which he could feel cracking. He wheezed and tried to suck in air. Najjar hit him again, this time in the shoulder, and Robert went down. His vision was blurry and he could feel himself slipping away. Najjar stood over him with the plank raised over his head, calculating the kill shot.

Robert concentrated the last of his strength and swept his leg as hard as he could at Najjar's ankles, bringing him down, his head hitting the ground near Robert's outstretched legs. Robert wrapped his legs around Najjar's neck in a headscissors hold and squeezed with as much pressure as he could, cutting off Najjar's air supply. Robert kept squeezing and squeezing with all his strength, which he felt was leaving him like a battery that was dying. Then, as Najjar began to turn blue, Robert's lights went completely out.

CHAPTER FIFTY

Robert's eyes came into focus on a stinging bright light, which, at first, seemed white hot. Then, the light withdrew and he realized he was in a hospital and that a doctor was looking in his eyes for signs of consciousness. He tried to move, but was restrained by a body cast. Robert could hear the doctor talking to somebody.

"You can have five minutes with him – that's all."

A nurse elevated his bed and Robert saw the two FBI agents who had accosted him in the storage parking lot in Las Vegas standing in front of his bed, along with another man he had never seen. The third man was dressed better than the other two, like an executive who worked for someone like Bryce Williamson.

One of the agents, Wokowski, spoke. "Do you want to explain how you were found next to the body of a dead terrorist?"

Robert's throat was dry, and the nurse gave him some water. He drank, then answered hoarsely, "Beats me."

"How did you get these injuries?"

"I fell."

The executive stood up and brushed Wokowski aside with his hand. "Enough of this bullshit, Garcia. You were found 12 miles from a foiled terrorist operation to blow up the nuclear reactors at Indian Point, next to the number two man of the Islamic State who was dead as a doornail, and you expect us to believe it's only a coincidence?"

"You can believe whatever you want. I don't really give a crap."

"Well maybe this will make you give a crap. At this point, Mr. Garcia, the facts are whatever I say they are. We have you next to Badi Hasib Najjar, the likely mastermind of the nuclear plant attack. He's dead, you're alive. You were one of his compatriots who participated in the attack and he died in the process of punishing you for your failure when you dared to fight him back."

Robert rolled his aching eyes. "That's the best you can come up with?"

"That and the courageous efforts of the trained security team at Indian Point."

"I see."

"So it goes like this, Garcia. I'm the director of the National Counterterrorism Center. We know what happened at Indian Point and are in a superior position to report the facts."

"You've got nothing on me."

"Except for killing Najjar."

"Never mind the fact that you would have done it yourself and I saved you the trouble, it was classic self-defense. That crazy bastard tried to smash my head in with a two-by-four."

"What would have motivated him to do that?"

"I don't know. Why don't you go to hell and ask him yourself?"

"Now, listen here, smartass. The evidence you claim we won't find against you, we will find it alright, and it'll put you right there at Indian Point among your comrades. One of them who's barely alive I'm sure will take great pleasure in identifying you."

"Knock yourself out."

"We can't have you out there anymore, running around, killing terrorists on American soil."

"I told you it was self-defense."

Anderson's face reddened. "God damn it, I'm not talking about Najjar and you know it! We're going to give you an offer you can't refuse. You'll have only two options."

"Are you Don Corleone or Monty Hall?"

Anderson ignored Robert's pun and barreled on. "Go to prison for the rest of your life or work for us offshore. If you work for us, you'll get full immunity for all your crimes."

"Except Phoenix," Samuels interrupted.

"Oh, yeah, there's a detective in Phoenix with a hard-on for you. We couldn't convince him to go along with the offer. But if you sign with us, you'll be so deep undercover he'll never find you."

"I already told Wokowski here what you could do with your offer. Don't you remember?"

"Maybe you'd better think long and hard about this before you snap back with a stupid answer like that."

"Maybe I should see my lawyer."

233

The doctor came back in, signaling that the interview was over by making a "cut" sign with his hand against his throat.

"You have 24 hours to decide. Agent Wokowski will leave you his number. Give him your decision before the time is up."

Anderson stormed out of the room. Wokowski put a business card on the tray next to Robert's bed and walked out with Samuels.

Robert thought again of his last thought in the struggle with Najjar. *He should have used a gun.*

CHAPTER FIFTY ONE

Jason Maynard's television was on as he ate a frozen TV dinner, listening to the news reports of the foiled attack on the Indian Point Energy Center in New York.

Highly trained security guards foiled a commando-style attempt by a group of heavily armed terrorists this morning at the Indian Point Nuclear Power Plant in Upstate New York. Had the two reactors been compromised, it could have caused contamination as far away as New York City. Reports are just coming in, but a spokesman for the New York State Police says 19 terrorists and 12 security guards were killed in the siege.

Maynard didn't believe the reports for a second. He wrote them off as stories planted by the government to control public perception. They didn't want anyone to know just how vulnerable critical facilities like nuclear and chemical plants really were and how faulty their security was. The Internet had its own take on the story and was already attributing the foiled attack to Paladine.

Maynard got on the phone to Wokowski, but was put into voice mail, so he left a message to call him back. They had claimed to have Robert Garcia in custody and wanted Joshua to go along with a ridiculous offer to give him immunity for the Phoenix murder. But they didn't mention anything about the nuclear plant attack. Maybe they had gone ahead and made their deal with Garcia without him.

Finally, on a rainy, muddy day in Phoenix, Maynard was able to connect with the agent in Washington.

"So whatever happened to the Garcia case?"

There was an uncomfortable pause on the bureaucratic end, then, "We've closed that case. Couldn't find any evidence to pin him to any of the murders."

"Sounds like you've stopped trying all of a sudden."

"What's there to do? We're happy there's no more vigilantes running around killing terrorists."

"And what about Garcia?"

"What about him? Maybe he's dead."

Reluctantly, Joshua moved on, but he would never stop working on the Garcia case and monitoring it for new developments. He kept up the visitations with his children and tried to be less obsessive about his work. That proved to be very difficult for him at times, but he knew he had to straighten out his priorities. Since splitting up with Cynthia, the kids had already grown and his son had grown apart from him. He made himself a "no work" policy during his weekends with the children, and only broke it once in a while.

Joshua took Erica to her dance classes on Tuesdays and Thursdays after work, and took Jim to soccer practice on Monday, Wednesday and Friday. He had made up his mind to be as good a visiting father as he was a policeman, even though the challenges for the former seemed overwhelming at times.

CHAPTER FIFTY TWO

In the days after the attack, left-wing politicians stepped up on their soapboxes and belied their right-wing opposition's claims that the United States was safe from terrorist attacks. The conservatives, whether they were elephants or donkeys, claimed that the fact the people were safe had been proven by the foiled Indian Point siege. The media reported the one-month anniversary of the attack, which gave the leaders another opportunity to tout their prowess, but after that, the incident was filed away in the public's memory banks until it eventually faded like it had been attacked by Alzheimer's disease. People went to work, paid their bills, had scx, fought with their spouses, and life went on.

The Paladine legend eventually faded into oblivion, like every urban fad had before it. The market for Paladine action figures had dried up, but not Joshua Maynard's interest in the case. Like the bloodhound he was, he kept following up on the only leads he had. When Maynard followed up on the only viable lead – the pet kennel in Las Vegas – they reported that the dog had not been claimed and had been sent to the pound.

Nathan Anderson received a pat on the back from the president, but recognition for the fiction he had concocted to cover up the attack on Indian Point wasn't what he really wanted. His agency was still as impotent as it ever was and he didn't see it becoming any more effective in the future. He continued to fight for the implementation of the changes called for in the Congressional Report, but, after the memory of the attack had faded, other priorities took a front seat over the War on Terror. Russia was the big enemy now. Fighting a foe of that magnitude called for massive defense expenditures.

The president did promise, however, to personally oversee the NCTC program and work with the other agencies to foster "cohesion and cooperation." He had made a lot of promises during the final part of his term, all empty, while he dreamed of golf and the good life that would be after his term was over. His work would then be what he enjoyed the most – public speaking – which would be more lucrative than being in office ever was.

CHAPTER FIFTY THREE

The cable cars were running the day Bryce Williamson threw his final punch against the Big C. People were streaming over the bridges into the city by the bay and scurrying along the sidewalks, heading for jobs, important business meetings, breakfast rendezvous – everyone was in a hurry to get somewhere. The markets in Chinatown had opened early before the fog had lifted when Bryce Williamson had taken his last breath. Life went on without missing a beat – or Williamson.

Bryce didn't want a funeral service. Pursuant to his last requests, his body was cremated and the urn buried in an unmarked grave with no graveside ceremony. His foundation, however, continued to exist in perpetuity, even without Paladine. Bryce's money lived on to pester politicians into promoting more effective ways to battle terrorism at home and abroad and provided grants to education programs in local mosques.

The few remaining employees at Bryce's home office pitched together to box up his personal belongings for charity. They were sad at his passing, but he had lived a full life and had not suffered long in the last days. Rationalization always seemed to justify death if the person was perceived to have had a "good life." When the movers came for the last stack of boxes, Jessica smiled at them.

"Is that it, ma'am?"

She paused, choked, put her fist to her lips, then replied, "Yes, yes, it's finished. Thank you."

They nodded and started to leave with the load of boxes.

"Wait."

The two men stopped and turned their heads, one with a look of curiosity on his face. Jessica pulled two fifty dollar bills out of her purse and gave one to each man.

A hush fell over the office after everyone else had left. Jessica spent her last hour of hire packing the things from her own desk. As she did, she reflected on the ten years she had worked for Bryce. He had always been good to her. A single tear escaped from the corner of her eye and ran down her cheek.

CHAPTER FIFTY FOUR

Las Vegas was an unforgiving town, a transient town. Whenever Virginia had succeeded in making a friend, the friend would invariably leave town, the result of a failed opportunity in Vegas or the appearance of another one elsewhere. She hadn't met any new men after Julio. She never really had the opportunity to get to know the strange man or figure out why she was so attracted to him, but she sometimes wondered what had become of him.

She felt lucky to have her job, as boring as it could be sometimes. It kept her hands busy and she liked talking to people. For her customers, the DMV was not a place where they preferred to spend their time. The challenge to Virginia was to pull a smile or two out of them with some friendly conversation, to make an otherwise unpleasant day a little more bearable.

She spent her off-time at home reading, speaking with her mother by telephone, and going to the gym to stay in shape.

On a cold winter afternoon, Virginia arrived home from work. She got out of her car, wrapped her scarf tightly around her neck as it blew in the icy wind, and walked a quick pace to her apartment, fishing in her purse for the keys as she scurried along. She stopped at the mailbox quickly and pulled out what could only be a stack of bills and junk mail, and headed upstairs to her apartment.

She escaped from the chilly gusts of wind through the door to her home and shed her jacket. Warm at last! Virginia threw down her purse, plopped on the couch and began looking through the junk mail. As she sorted through the bills, leaving them unopened for payday, she noticed an envelope from the John Williamson Foundation to Fight Terrorism. Thinking it to be another call for a charitable donation which she could ill afford because she had already committed herself to too many, she almost threw it into the wastebasket. But her curiosity got the better of her and she opened it up and her eyes opened wide at the contents – a check, made out to her, for five hundred thousand dollars. Virginia fell back on the divan with her hand against her heart, and looked at the check again to make sure it wasn't one of those phony sweepstakes checks. Why was she chosen for this gift? She had nothing to do with fighting terrorism. That thought was immediately replaced by dreams of the life that money could make possible. Thank God she wasn't a gambler!

CHAPTER FIFTY FIVE

It was the city that time had forgotten since the Crusades. A city with no running water. That was provided by the ISIS water tankers and was used for drinking and preparing meals. With no gas, cooking became a historical artifact. Bathing was an unheard of luxury. The electricity worked a few minutes every day, if the residents were lucky. The heads of the statues in Naeem Square had been knocked off. Human heads from public executions adorned the tops of the fences in their place. In the square, stoning, beheading and crucifixion had become a normal occurrence. Many of the city's historical structures had been destroyed by ISIS. Many of the others had been bombed into oblivion. This was Raqqa, the proud capital of the Islamic State.

Outside the city, in a secret safe-house, Abdul-Fattah Zamani, the head of the ISIS immigration committee, responsible for smuggling fighters across the Turkish border into Syria, sipped his tea as he made notes for his meeting with Abu Bakr al-Baghdadi.

Outside, a convoy of pickup trucks full of fighters with mounted machine guns and an armored Humvee pulled up. It was Zamani's ride. As an assistant packed up his things, he rose and went to the window to look outside. That was usually someone else's job, but he never trusted it to chance. It only took one second to check. Seeing that everything was clear, he breathed a sigh of relief.

The shot was followed a fraction of a second later by the tinkling sound of the glass window being penetrated by a bullet. Zamani grasped at his throat in a futile attempt to stop the pressure flow of arterial blood and fell to the floor. His assistants came to his aid. One ran outside and screamed for a medic. The fighters in his convoy came to life and began shooting wildly into the distance.

Robert Garcia left his Dragunov SVD sniper rifle on its bipod and slipped out of the half destroyed, abandoned house. He walked along the streets at a regular pace, blending into the crowd of villagers in broad daylight. At the corner, he calmly opened the door of a waiting pickup which took him away from the village and on to another assignment. Robert reached back into the back seat to the big dummy sitting back there, panting from the heat and whining with glee to see him. He scratched him behind the ears and smiled.

AFTERWORD

When I began this novel, it was supposed to be my attempt to write a "normal" assassination thriller. However, when I got into the research I was shocked. I knew there had to be radicalized jihadists living in the United States because the FBI has arrested many of them in sting operations.[3] [4] However, there is evidence, readily available from Internet sources, that Sheik Mubarak Ali Jilani, a sheik from Pakistan, a suspected terrorist the US government alleges is the founder of the terrorist organization, *Jamaat ul-Fuqra*[5], is also the

---

[3] Pfeiffer, Alex, 31 Suspected ISIS Terrorists Have Been Arrested in the U.S. In the Past Year, The Daily Caller, August 6, 2016

[4] Goldman, Adam, The Islamic State's suspected inroads into America, The Washington Post, August 8, 2016

[5] Bocuher, Richard, Daily Press Briefing, United States Dept. of State, March 27, 2002

founder of Muslims of America, Inc. (MOA).[6] which has been accused of establishing jihad training compounds in the states which are classified by law enforcement as "classically structured terrorist cells." [7] A storage locker maintained by ul Fuqra in Colorado Springs was raided by local police in 1989, who found a cache of firearms, grenades, plastic explosives and target practice silhouettes labeled "Zionist Pig" and "FBI Anti-Terrorist Squad."[891011]

Claims have been made by the anti-Islamic group, Christian Action Network[12] that the MOA trains men and women to be jihadists and to take action upon Gilani's

---

[6] Mauro, Ryan, Muslims of the Americas (MOA), The Clarion Project, February 12, 2013

[7] Brown, Carol, Muslims of America training compounds, American Thinker, September 20, 2015

[8] Hossenball, Mark, Another Holy War, Waged on American Soil, Newsweek, February 28, 1994

[9] Mauro, Ryan, Muslims of the Americas (MOA), The Clarion Project, February 12, 2013

[10] Brown, Carol, Muslims of America training compounds, American Thinker, September 20, 2015

[11] The Blaze, For the Record, Sleeper Cells Inside Our Nation?, Febraury 19, 2014

[12] Is There a Muslim Terrorist Training Camp Near You?, The Conservative Papers, May 7, 2013

order.[13] Reports by the Anti-Defamation League indicate that the group's emails and websites have featured writings by anti-Semites and Holocaust deniers and advocates jihadist violence.[14]

The National Counterterrorism Center (NCTC) was established in 2004 to serve as the primary organization in collecting and analyzing all intelligence pertaining to terrorism possessed or acquired by the US government.[15] However, according to a 2011 Congressional Report, it could be more effective.

"Arguably most important, however, is the capability of ensuring that analysts are integrated into the counterterrorism effort, that operational planning is shared with analytical offices so that particular reactions or threats can be anticipated and assessed. The most important "wall" may not be the one that existed between law enforcement and intelligence agencies prior to 2001, but the one that often persists between analysts and operators. The latter may lack the time and opportunity to integrate analytical efforts into their ongoing work, but if the country is aiming for a "zero defects" approach to terrorism, close attention to intelligence is a prerequisite. Some experienced observers maintain that "zero defects" is unrealizable, some failures are inevitable and argue that it is more responsible to minimize failures and limit their effects. The use of intelligence by policymakers

---

[13] Brown, Carol, Muslims of America training compounds, American Thinker, September 20, 2015

[14] Muslims of the Americas: In Their Own Words, Anti - Defamation League, http://archive.adl.org/extremism/moa/

[15] NCTC website: https://www.nctc.gov/index.html

and military commanders is in largest measure the responsibility of the Executive Branch, but some observers argue that the quality of analysis may be enhanced when analytical efforts are regularly reviewed by congressional committees and hearings are conducted to ensure that they are properly prepared and fully used."[16]

President Obama held a briefing with his national security team at the NCTC in December 2015[17] but it was a largely symbolic measure, resulting in no change in policy.

There is a growing threat from the so-called "lone-wolf" attacks, such as we have seen in Nice on July 14, 2016 and other parts of Europe, but there are also jihadists recruiters for the Islamic State, Al-Qaeda, Hamas and Nusra using social media to connect with potential jihadists for financing and soldiering right here in the United States.[18]

---

[16] Best, Richard A., The National Counterterrorism Center (NCTC) Responsibilities and Potential Congressional Concerns, December 19, 2011, Congressional Research Service

[17] White House, Office of Press Secretary, Statement by the President After Briefing at National Counterterrorism Center, December 17, 2015

[18] Bardin, Jeff, What it's like to be recruited by ISIS online, May 22, 2015, Business Insider

What is alarming is that most of the recruits are young people; many of them teenagers.[19] The turbulent teenage years are known for philosophical reflectiveness on the meaning of life (or lack thereof). Despair and even suicide is a common solution that some young people resort to instead of facing their problems. ISIS has tapped into these feelings of Muslim youths, some of whom have bought in to their propaganda and go on to serve the Islamic State by fighting in Syria, or answering the call to kill infidels in their own backyard. Suddenly, suicide becomes a more complicated problem, with often more than one victim.

While enforcement efforts are disjointed, disconnected, and have not evolved to address the threats, the real solution can only be found in social change. Unfortunately, young people often turn to their peers instead of authority, and this can be a problem. In the case of the Islamic State, the recruiters come disguised as peers. Not only is education important, but enlightenment as well. The young people of the millennial generation are lost. Their prospects for gainful employment, even with education are bleak, and they are struggling to find the purpose to their lives while the elites in the establishment continue to make disastrous interventionist foreign policy which gave rise to the power of the Islamic State, and then pulled out the military force too soon, leaving a tremendous gap of power that ISIS was only too glad to fill up.

Vigilantism is not the answer. The government feels free to disregard its laws and principles and continues to use assassination abroad as a technique to deter the spread of the

---

[19] Geiger, Gloria, This is How ISIS Uses Social Media to Recruit American Teens, November 20, 2015, Teen Vogue

Islamic State, but whether it is with drones or teams of Navy Seals, or lone CIA assassins, a program of targeted killing is not going to solve the problem and does nothing more than give the politicians something to brag about in the next election.

One more thing...

I hope you have enjoyed this book and I am thankful that you have spent the time to get to this point, which means that you must have received something from reading it. I would be honored if you would post your thoughts, and also leave a review on Amazon. Just go to the landing page of the book: https://amzn.com/B01KKXBP32 and scroll down to the button "leave a customer review) to leave your review.

Best regards,

Kenneth Eade

info@kennetheade.com

BONUS OFFER

Sign up for paperback discounts, advance sale notifications of this and other books and free stuff by visiting my website, http://www.kennetheade.com/free-download/. I will never spam you.

OTHER BOOKS BY KENNETH EADE

Brent Marks Legal Thriller Series

A Patriot's Act

Predatory Kill

HOA Wire

Unreasonable Force

Killer.com

Absolute Intolerance

The Spy Files

Decree of Finality

Beyond All Recognition

Involuntary Spy Espionage Series

An Involuntary Spy

To Russia for Love

Stand Alone

Terror on Wall Street

Non-fiction

Bless the Bees: The Pending Extinction of our
Pollinators and What You Can Do to Stop It

A, Bee, See: Who are our Pollinators and Why are They
in Trouble?

Save the Monarch Butterfly

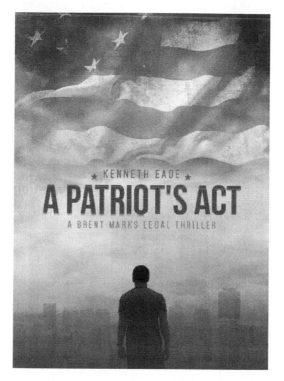

CHAPTER ONE

Ahmed felt the butt of the rifle strike his spine between his shoulder blades as his knees buckled, and he hit the floor. The sensation of falling was even stranger because he couldn't see anything. It was as if he were in slow motion, spiraling out of control.

His hands were shackled behind his back, so there was no way to break his fall. He landed on his side, slamming his shoulder into the cold concrete floor. He could feel the fibers of the black hood against his lips, and smell the sweat of the last person who had been forced to wear it. He stood up and started to walk again.

"Move faster Haji!" commanded an authoritative voice in a Southern American drawl. Ahmed felt the rifle butt hit hard against his spine again and he shuffled faster, within the confines of his ankle chains, which allowed only a minimum of movement. Thoughts of his wife Catherine, her silky brown hair, soft brown eyes and captivating smile, and their two small children, Karen and Cameron, back in their home in Santa Barbara, flooded his brain. These thoughts were the only thing lately that kept him sane.

"Up against the wall! – Stop there! Up against the wall I said – now!"

Ahmed stopped and did as he was commanded.

"Listen up!" barked a mechanical voice in the darkness, "My name is Sergeant Brown. You have been placed in my custody. You're here because you have refused to cooperate in interrogations. The decision has been made to execute you by firing squad."

"Wait!" said Ahmed, "I'm an American citizen."

"Sure you are, A-hab."

"My name is Ahmed."

"Your name is A-hab. A-hab the A-rab and the only thing I need to hear from you today is whether you want your mask on or off."

"Off."

Ahmed felt the black bag ripped from his head and, for the first time, faced his aggressors. The man who had ripped off his bag was a young man in military camouflage fatigues, holding an M16 to his chest. In front of him was an eight-man firing squad, also in camouflage fatigues, with rifles at their sides in ready position. Standing at their side was obviously Sergeant Brown, a hefty black man with huge hands, the only one not holding a weapon. For a 25-year-old man like Brown, who was always inept in every way outside the service, power was orgasmic. He basked in it like the sun, as if he was on a white sand beach in Maui.

Brown was proud to be in the United States Army, the finest military service of the greatest country in the world, a beacon for freedom, the leader of the New World Order. The Army was his life, a life that had so much more depth, meaning and importance than it did before. He was entrusted with the valuable task of shaping young men and women under his charge to destroy the enemy and wipe terrorism from the planet. The enemy was the low-life, stinking Arabs, those sand niggers, the little maggots who had strapped bombs to themselves and had blown his comrades to bits in Iraq. They were like a disease, a plague that had to be wiped out.

"I have the right to talk to an attorney," Ahmed pleaded.

"You what? You don't have any rights, A-hab," said Brown, "You're a terrorist. The only right you have is to choose to wear the mask or not, and you already exercised that right."

The young soldier fastened a leather strap around Ahmed's waist, pinning his spine to a wooden post. He turned his head to look behind himself at the canvas wall, pocked with gunshots. The soldier then strapped his ankles to the post.

"Please, let me call my lawyer. This is all a big mistake!"

"Yeah, yeah, a big mistake. I've heard that one before. All you fucking Hajis say the same goddamn thing – it's programmed. You should have cooperated when we asked about your superiors in Al-Qaeda."

"I don't know anyone in Al-Qaeda."

"Don't bullshit me, boy!"

Brown, like a machine, pivoted, walked a few paces, and then pivoted again, so he was face to face with Ahmed, took a piece of paper from his pocket, unfolded it and recited in a military monotone, "You have been found guilty of terrorism. The penalty is death by firing squad. Do you have any last statement?"

"But I…"

"I repeat, do you have any last statement?"

"Yes, please, I want to cooperate, I really do, but I don't know what you want from me. I don't know anything!"

The young man with the M16 then approached Ahmed, pinned a white heart onto his chest, and moved back. Brown marched off to the right of the firing squad.

Sweat was dripping into Ahmed's eyes, stinging them. He said a silent prayer, thought about his wife and children, then looked at Brown with defiant eyes.

"I'm not a terrorist. I am an American citizen. I have the right, like any other American citizen, to a lawyer and a trial before any execution. I have been denied these rights. You will answer to God for your crimes."

"To hell with your rights, boy. We got all the rights here," said Brown, who raised his arm and shouted, "READY!"

The eight marksmen cocked their rifles.

"AIM!"

The eight pointed their rifles at Ahmed, who shivered uncontrollably. His knees gave way and he hung on the post like a man crucified.

"FIRE!"

The deafening explosion of the eight rifles was the last thing Ahmed heard. He felt the bullets hit his flesh and his body crumpled forward, hanging lifelessly from the post like a scarecrow.

CHAPTER TWO

Catherine Khury sat in the plain-wrap waiting room of the FBI's Santa Barbara field office, fidgeting in her purse for her phone. *Hold it together, Cate!* she told herself. She had been living in hell the past few weeks. She was an attractive woman, but her ordeal made every one of her 30 years appear as if she had lived her life without sleeping. She looked at the time. Only five minutes had passed since the last time she had checked. A friendly looking, pretty young woman entered the room.

"Hello, ma'am, I'm Agent Wollard," the woman said, extending her hand, which Catherine shook.

"Catherine Khury."

"Would you please come in?"

Catherine sat in a small steel and vinyl black chair and Agent Wollard behind an aluminum desk with a false wood veneer surface.

"How can I help you, Mrs. Khury?"

"My husband, Ahmed, is missing." Catherine's bottom lip began to quiver, as she fought back tears. She had to remain strong; strong for her husband, and especially for her children.

"Mrs. Khury, we don't really look for missing persons here at the FBI."

"That's not what I heard."

"Well, we do maintain a database of missing persons, but unless it's a child, and foul play is suspected, we don't really get actively involved."

"Agent Wollard, I don't know where else to go. My husband and his brother have been missing since my husband went to Iraq to help him."

"Your husband is in Iraq?"

"The last I heard. But nobody has seen or heard from him in days," Catherine sobbed, struggling to keep her composure.

Angela handed her a tissue from the box on her desk. "Is your husband a United States citizen?"

"Yes, he has been for many years."

The tears finally made their way over the spill gates, and Catherine emptied them into the tissue.

"Have you tried to find him in Iraq?"

"Yes, but the only person I know there is his brother and he's not answering. I don't have anyone else to call."

"Well, the best I can do is to take a missing persons report and make a couple of phone calls."

"Would you please?" Catherine felt instant relief. Even though this Agent Wollard didn't promise a solution, just having any kind of help made her feel less hopeless.

"Yes, of course. Please, fill out these forms and, when you're done, I can enter the information into our missing person's database."

"Thank you Agent Wollard."

"I'm sorry I couldn't do more."

***

After Mrs. Khury left, Angela processed the report, and then called Bill Thompson, one of her contacts in Washington.

"Bill, I've got a missing persons case that I may need your help on."

"Since when does the bureau really ever work a missing person's case?"

Angela chuckled. "I've been known to do it from time to time. Listen, he's an Iraqi born, US citizen, who went to Iraq last month and nobody has heard from him in about a week. His wife is worried to death."

"Send me an email and I'll make some calls."

"Thanks Bill."

CHAPTER THREE

Ahmed opened his eyes to complete blackness. *Am I alive?* Panicking, he put his hand in front of his face and he couldn't see it. He moved his fingers. Still nothing. Ahmed's frantic eyes moved back and forth and there was not a sliver of light. *I'm blind,* he thought. A sudden surge of adrenalin compelled him to action. His brain sent a signal to stand up and, as he did, the pain shot from his feet to his head like a hammer hit on a high striker in a carnival. Gravity pulled his broken body to his knees and he collapsed. He felt his body: No clothing.

What happened? Am I dead?

No, he thought, *I must be alive.* He was in too much pain to be dead. He felt his chest for bullet wounds, but found none. Except for some tender spots on his chest and back and some scrapes on his knees, there was nothing. *They must have used rubber bullets.*

Ahmed strained to see, but it was no use. He felt his face: It was swollen and bruised. *They must have blinded me in the shooting,* he thought. As his other four senses came to life, he realized that he was sore all over. He tried to stand again, but his legs would not cooperate. He felt them with his new eyes; the bones felt straight and unbroken. *Must be sprains, but why am I blind?* He struggled to control the panic and the terror. *Think, think. Have to think.*

Ahmed crawled on his hands and knees and propped himself up against the wall, which was as cold and damp as the floor. He felt along the walled boundaries of his confinement. *One, two, three, four, five, six, about seven feet in one direction. One, two, three, four, about five feet in the other direction.* Next, he negotiated the circumference on his hands and knees.

How did he get himself into this mess? From his cozy home in Santa Barbara, to the battered and occupied Baghdad, to this. His brother, Sabeen needed his help, so he went. It was as simple as that. The next events were a blur to him; The raid, his capture. Now he was in some kind of military prison.

Since his capture, Ahmed had been stripped naked, cavity searched, shaved bald, beaten, kicked and spat on. And then the mock execution. It made his current confinement in this dark cage somewhat of a relief, not at all what it was designed for. The walls were as cold as a headstone. He felt around them until he came to a steel door.

He thought of his wife, Catherine. She must know he was missing by now. But even if he was to be rescued, what good is a blind husband? An accountant by trade, there was no way he could work with figures as a blind man. He would be a complete burden on the entire family. *The best thing to do is to kill myself,* he thought. He had some life insurance, and wondered if it would pay off in the event of his suicide.

* * *

The time passed, but Ahmed had no way of measuring it. *How long have I been like this?* Ahmed concentrated on his other senses, but there was no input, save the sound of the pounding of his own heart. His mouth was as dry as a slab of jerky, so he tried to wet his broken lips with his tongue. In despair, he dropped to the floor. Lying there on his back, he rubbed his eyes and, suddenly, he saw tiny stars above him in the blackness. *Light! I can see light!*

The tiny stars spread out in a geometric pattern, like symbols in a matrix. *Those can't be stars. They're not random.* Ahmed's accountant's brain analyzed the patterns of light, but then they turned into eyes, angrily staring at him. *Stop! Stop! Please, somebody help me!* Then the eyes pulled back to reveal a miniature firing squad, with their rifles trained on Ahmed. He heard the blast of their rifles, almost in slow motion, and felt the bullets ripping through his flesh as his brain switched off.

ABOUT THE AUTHOR

Author Kenneth Eade, best known for his legal and political thrillers, practiced law for 30 years before publishing his first novel, "An Involuntary Spy." Eade, an up-and-coming author in the legal thriller and courtroom drama genre, has been described by critics as "one of our strongest thriller writers on the scene, and the fact that he draws his stories from the contemporary philosophical landscape is very much to his credit." Critics have also said that "his novels will remind readers of John Grisham, proving that Kenneth Eade deserves to be on the same lists with the world's greatest thriller authors."

Says Eade of the comparisons: "John Grisham is famous for saying that sometimes he likes to wrap a good story around an important issue. In all of my novels, the story and the important issues are always present."

Eade is known to keep in touch with his readers, offering free gifts and discounts to all those who sign up at his website, www.kennetheade.com.